Moon Ridge

Valley

Moon Ridge

Valley

Broken Promises

by

Ashley Davis

Printed in the United States of America

First Printing, 2020

ISBN: 978-1-951883-20-1

Butterfly Typeface Publishing
PO Box 56193
Little Rock, AR 72215

This book is dedicated to all of the readers of

the Moon Ridge Valley series.

"Riley, are you seriously asking me to

homecoming?

Table of Contents

Introduction

"Hi Sheriff, what are you doing back so soon?" Reagan asked hoping to hear some good news.

"When my deputies called to inform me that Skye was back in town, I hopped on the first flight."

"I'm assuming you still didn't find Logan, sir."

Before he could answer, a deputy knocked on the door.

"Excuse me, Sheriff. I'm sorry to bother you, but the state troopers have arrived with the assailant. Also, they brought what they found in her trunk. I think it's something you'll want to see." The deputy turned and walked out of the door.

"Excuse me, kids. I'll be back momentarily."
Sheriff Franklin walked out of his office
leaving us to wonder what was in Skye's
trunk.

He was gone for about ten minutes before he
returned with some bad news. "Skye's trunk
was filled with blood. The DNA test came
back. It was a match for Logan. No one could
survive losing that much blood. I'm sorry, but
Logan is dead."

My worst fear had come true. I ran out of the
Sheriff's Office in panic. I wasn't paying
attention to where I was going, and that's
when it hit me.

Chapter One

"Ouch! Get off of me!" I yelled at the guy who jumped on top of me. However, my annoyance quickly turned to gratitude when a car flew by me as it barreled down the road. "How did I not see that coming? I'm sorry for flipping out on you."

"It's ok; I'm sure a beautiful girl like you has been hit on before, but not like this." He said chuckling.

"Not to be rude, but can you get off of me?" I replied uncomfortably.

"Oh wow, I'm sorry. I didn't even realize. Let me help you up." He stretched out his hand and said, "My name is Cody. It's nice to meet you."

"I'm Riley. It's nice to meet you too."

Well, Riley, I'm sure I'll see you around." He walked away and disappeared into the distance.

"Riley! Are you ok?" My friends asked frantically.

"I'm fine. Please just take me home."

"Not before we take you to the doctor." Reagan said with a concerned tone.

I would have argued, but I was a little banged up from hitting the road.

The trip to the doctor's office was silent. We all were mourning the loss of Logan. In my mind, I knew he was gone, but my heart did not want to accept it. Logan had been a part of my life for most of my life. I wasn't sure I would ever be able to let him go. I remained silent until after the appointment was over.

"Riley, we're all sad that Logan is gone. We know you need some time to grieve, but you can't just shut everyone out. He wouldn't want you to do that." I knew Reagan was trying to be helpful, but I really didn't care. As much as I didn't want to admit it, I couldn't get past the fact that Logan died trying to rescue Reagan. If Logan hadn't done that for me, he would still be here. No one else understood how I felt, and no one was going to understand.

"Thank you for that Reagan. I'll try to cheer up while I'm with you guys, but do me a favor and drop me home as quickly as possible."

Reagan never listened to me when he thought he knew what was best. He dropped everyone else off except for me.

"Reagan, what are you doing? I asked you to take me home."

"I know, but I'm not taking you home. You don't need to be alone right now."

He took me to High Pointe Peak. I was enraged because High Pointe Peak was the last place I needed and wanted to be.

"Reagan, why are we here? You need to take me home immediately!"

"Look, Riley, I brought you here to give you a chance to clear your head. I remember you telling me something a few months back."

I stared at him blankly.

"You said you do your best thinking under the stars; you also said it makes you feel comfortable."

Deep down, I knew he was right, but that was irrelevant.

"Fine, whatever."

We sat on a bench that looked over the city. Everything was breathtaking in the moonlight. For a moment, I was able to forget about my problems.

"Thank you, Reagan. I'm sorry I took my frustration out on you."

"Trust me; I get it. I still don't understand why anyone would go after my parents, so I know the frustration."

He put his arm around me, and I didn't push him away. I hated the fact that I was in love with two completely different guys. Sure, they both had their quirks and failings, but there was something special about them.

Still, in love or not, that was the last thing on which I needed to focus. We sat on the bench for several hours in silence. It was exactly what I needed. Although it didn't change my circumstances, it did give me time to decompress. Time had flown by, and we both had to go home. Reagan dropped me off, and I thanked him for everything.

That morning when I woke up, I decided to go into town to the Sheriff's station. I walked in and was surprised to find the boy who had saved me the day before.

"Hey Riley, what are you doing here? Are you feeling any better?"

"I'm ok, Cody. I could ask you the same."

"I'm checking to see if there are any updates on my cousin. My family and I moved here after school let out, but when we got here, we learned that my cousin was missing. We've been doing all we can to find him since we've been here."

As he spoke, I remembered that Logan had a cousin named Cody who used to hang out with us during summer vacations when Logan and I were younger, but it couldn't be him.

"What's your cousin's name, Cody?"

"Logan, Logan Andrews."

"Oh my word! Cody? Is that really you?"

"Wait a minute! You're not the same Riley that is best friends with my cousin? You look so different!"

"So, do you. You said you moved here?"

"Yes, not that long ago," he said looking a little antsy.

In all the time we spent talking, I realized that neither of us had done what we went there to do.

"It was great catching up with you, but we both need to see if there's any update on Logan."

"Hi Cody, hi Riley, I'm assuming you're here to see if any more information has turned up about Logan." Sheriff Franklin said as he walked out of his office.

"Yes sir, we're really hoping you have some good news for us." Cody said looking hopeful.

"Actually, last night we interrogated Skye, and some new information did turn up."

We stared at him waiting to hear what happened, but he said nothing further and walked away. Nevertheless, we followed behind him.

"Sheriff, will you please tell us what's going on?" I begged.

"I am on my way to see the Andrews. You both are welcome to come if they are ok with it." Sheriff Franklin replied.

I had jogged from my house, so I decided to ride with Cody since he offered. We weren't sure what to expect. All of the news any of us had received so far was bad, and with the police concluding that Logan was dead, the news couldn't get any worse. The car ride was quiet, and there was a lot of tension in the air. It was still hard to believe that Logan was gone. As we sat in silence, I made a decision. If the Sheriff had bad news, I was going to let go of Logan and move on with my life. I was in love with him, but I was also in love with Reagan. Logan had sacrificed himself for me, and I would always love him. Still, I knew he would want me to move on and more importantly, to be happy. As we pulled up to the Andrews' house, I took a deep breath and prepared myself for what was to come.

When we walked into the house, the Andrews and Sheriff Franklin were sitting in the living room waiting for us.

"Cody, Riley, come in and take a seat." Mrs. Andrews said trying her best to smile.

We thanked her and waited for the news.

Sheriff Franklin sat back, cleared his throat, and said, "Last night, we interrogated Skye. We offered her a deal for information. She admitted that Logan was in her trunk and that he was bleeding when he was put in there. However, most of the blood resulted from his escape. He was able to kick the taillights loose, but from what we could see, he cut himself opening the trunk. I believe Logan could still be alive, but he won't last much longer without medical attention. Skye didn't pursue him for that very reason."

Mrs. Andrews was crying hysterically by the time Sheriff Franklin finished what he was saying. I couldn't figure out if she was crying because there was a chance he was alive or because she was sure he was dead. Either way, I knew that my gut was right. Logan was alive, but I was nervous that he might not be for long.

The conversation moved to the dining room, so I decided to slip out of the front door. Cody followed me.

"Riley, are you all right? You seem upset, but I'm not sure why."

"I'm happy that there's hope, but I can't shake the feeling that the Logan who left won't be the one who returns.

Chapter Two

Senior year was almost here, and I couldn't imagine starting it without Logan. There were so many thoughts running through my head. Logan and I had mapped out senior year when we were in middle school. We would join yearbook. We would run for president and vice president of the class. More importantly, we were going to go to prom and graduate together.

Logan was the half to my whole, and without him, I felt like I was no longer living. I was just existing. Although I was sad that he was still gone, I knew I had to move on and start living my life again. Albeit, I was still in love with Logan, but that wasn't an option for me, at least not right now. Nevertheless, Reagan was here, and I had rekindled an old friendship with an old friend, Cody. It's not like I was alone, but I was feeling lonely. I wasn't sure what the year would bring, but I was hoping it would bring, clarity, peace of mind, and most of all, happiness.

Logan had now been missing for over two months. I had lost all hope that he would return. I wanted him to be ok, but enough time had passed that I was sure he wasn't ok. However, that couldn't be my focus. He couldn't be my focus. There were only a few days until the first day of school. I had spent so much time wallowing and stressing out that I had alienated almost all of my friends who were still here. Everyone had made a genuine effort to be there for me even though I wasn't receptive. I was sure that they were understanding since Logan and I had been best friends since Pre-K, but that still didn't excuse me choosing to ignore my friends all summer long. Regardless, both Cody and

Reagan had told me not to worry about how I had treated my other friends. They explained that true friends would still be there in the end, and that's what I was counting on.

I spent the next few days preparing for school. I was a senior now, and I needed to make sure I made an impression on the first day. Since my parents considered me to be responsible and they didn't feel like taking me school shopping, my mom and dad decided to get me a credit card with a low limit. With my new credit card, I was able to get everything I needed for school while still having money to spare.

Later that night, Cody came to pick me up. We had been spending a lot of time together, and I really enjoyed it. It also didn't hurt that we had a lot in common. A new restaurant had opened in town, and Cody wanted to take me there as an official kick-off to the beginning of the year. I would never tell him, but I was glad he had moved to Moon Ridge Valley. I was even happier that we were going to be seniors together.

"Hey Ry, are you ready for senior year?"

"Not really, but I'm sure it will be great!"

"Are you nervous about starting over at a new school for your senior year?"

Cody chuckled and flaunted his macho bravado as per usual. "Nervous? I'm never nervous, Ry. I have confidence to spare if you need some."

I shook my head and rolled my eyes at him. Nevertheless, I couldn't help but laugh. He was always so over the top, but that was the thing I liked about him most. When I was with him, it felt like my problems all disappeared, but that quickly came to an end when Reagan walked into the restaurant with some girl on his arm. I tried not to let it bother me, but I couldn't help but wonder who she was. However, I didn't want Cody to see that I was preoccupied.

"Cody, tonight has been really fun, and I don't want it to end. Can we go somewhere and talk or grab dessert?"

"Uh...yeah...sure, are you all right?" Cody clearly knew something was wrong, but I had no intention of telling him what had caused the change in my disposition.

"I'm fine. I'm great actually! I just really want some ice cream or cheesecake."

"Hmmm, it's fine if you don't want to tell me. We can go, but if you want, we can say hi to Reagan." Cody smirked knowingly.

I hated it when he smirked that way, and he knew it which made him enjoy it that much more. I remained silent because my facial expression said enough. We walked out of the restaurant and never said a word to Reagan. I don't think he even knew we were there.

After we left Picante y Fresco, Cody took me downtown to Icey Crème, the best dessert shop in the area. We decided to take a walk around the strip. It was always so interesting watching everyone interact. I was so busy watching everyone that I wasn't paying attention to where I was going. I tripped and almost landed face-first on the sidewalk, but Cody caught me just in time. I felt like he had swept me off my feet, and at that moment, everything changed. We looked into each other's eyes and drew closer until I heard a familiar voice calling my name.

"Riley! Hey Riley! I want to introduce you to someone!" Reagan yelled as he came running toward us.

I could see the disappointment on Cody's face. Our moment had come and gone, and we were back to reality.

"Hey Riley, Cody, I hope I didn't interrupt anything, but I wanted to introduce you to my best friend, Cassie."

I smiled and introduced myself, but I could tell that Reagan had not only interrupted us on purpose, but he had also followed us. I found it really strange that Reagan had never mentioned this so-called "best friend" until now. I didn't know anything about her, but I knew I didn't like her. I especially didn't like the way she was looking at Cody, and I didn't like the way Reagan was looking at her. Those were my boys, and I was not having a repeat of junior year with Omar, Zander, Logan, and Reagan. That almost ruined my friendships with them, and I was not willing to risk losing Cody or Reagan given that Logan was gone. I had grown weary of the turn the night had taken.

"Cassie, it was nice meeting you. Reagan, it was nice seeing you, but I really need to get home. I'll see you around." I could not wait to go home. I hoped that Cassie would only be in town for a brief stint and that things would return to normal or as normal as they could get.

Cody knew I was upset, and he was always willing to listen. Nonetheless, I didn't feel like talking.

"Riley, what's going on? You've been acting really strange tonight."

I looked at him, smiled, and remained quiet. I appreciated that he cared, but that's not what I needed right now.

"Riles, are we going to talk about what happened between us tonight?"

"Nope," I said as I turned and stared out of the window.

As soon as we pulled up to my house, I quickly hopped out of his car, said "Bye," and ran inside. I did not want to be bothered with questions of why I acted how I acted when I was out with Cody. All I wanted to do was crawl into bed with a tub of ice cream and cry while watching my favorite tv show.

Since school was starting in two days, I decided to have some alone time to regroup. I didn't go anywhere or talk to anyone which was rather easy because I had finished all of my school shopping. I also made sure to turn off my phone because no one could get upset if my phone was "dead." I spent time preparing myself for the drama I knew would unfold when I walked through the doors of Moon Ridge High.

Chapter Three

The first day of my senior year was finally here, and I could not be more excited! I couldn't wait to see everyone, but just as I suspected, drama was awaiting my arrival.

When I walked through the doors and saw all of my friends, my face lit up. However, it was strange that they were all talking to each other like the best of friends. It had never been that way before because the only thing they really had in common was me. Still, I was just happy to see them.

"Hey, guys!"

"Oh, hey Riley," Brie said a little lackluster.

"Hey Riley, have you met Reagan's best friend Cassie?" Zander asked mischievously.

"Yeah, hi Cassie, so you go here now?"

"I do. I transferred from Clear Falls High." She said smiling from ear to ear.

"Isn't it weird being at a new school with a bunch of people you don't know for your senior year?" I tried my best to hide my irritation and to act concerned.

"I thought it would be a little weird, but having my Reagy and meeting his friends has put me at ease."

I thought to myself. "Reagy? Reagy? Really? Ugh!" I just wanted to punch her in the face. She seemed to know exactly what to say to get under my skin. Nonetheless, I responded, "That's great!"

Everyone parted ways to go to class. I think they all knew I was upset, or they thought I was jealous with the exception of Reagan. As I sat in class watching the two of them, my blood started to boil. Who was this girl that showed up, captivated my friends, and stole the attention of my Reagan? Well, that was just it. He wasn't my Reagan. He wasn't anything more than my friend, and I was the one who decided things should be that way. I gazed off into the distance as my mind reeled. Reagan might have been preoccupied, but I had something good going with Cody, or at least, that's what I thought. What I didn't know was that Cody noticed my staring at Reagan and Cassie. Cody also saw the change in my mood and attitude when I was around the two of them, and although he liked me, he wasn't willing to share my heart with someone else. The first day of school wasn't even halfway finished, and I had already lost both of the guys in whom I was interested.

The rest of the day went by quickly. We all ate lunch together and planned to meet after school. We went to our favorite pizza place, Giana's Quick Fixin's. While we ate, Cassie told us stories of life in Clear Falls. The more stories she told, the more interesting she turned out to be. I wanted so badly to hate her, but I couldn't. I actually liked her, and it made sense why Reagan liked her as well. She was fun and carefree. She always had a smile on her face and genuinely seemed concerned about other people. I couldn't hate her if I tried.

"Reagan, can I talk to you for a moment?"

"Uh…sure." Reagan excused himself from the table, and we stepped outside to talk. As I looked over my shoulder, I saw Cassie's eyes following Reagan as he followed me.

"Reagan, I'm sorry for how I acted last night and earlier today. I'm glad you have Cassie, and I'm glad she has you. You guys make a good couple."

"Couple? What are you talking about, Riley?"

"Um…you and Cassie!"

"Cassie and I are not a couple. She's my best friend. That's all she is. Plus, why would you care anyway? You've been dating Cody for months now."

"Cody and I are not dating."

I turned to walk back inside, but Reagan grabbed my arm and said, "Don't walk away from me, Riley. You didn't answer my question."

I hated it when Reagan sounded intimidating. I knew he wouldn't hurt me, but it still made me uncomfortable. "You know why I care, Reagan."

"No, I really don't. We barely spent any time together all summer, but every time I turned around, you were with Cody. So, what's the deal?"

As I listened to Reagan, I came to realize why I was avoiding him. Nevertheless, I didn't want to hurt him, and I didn't want him to hate me. So, I lied. "I'm sorry. You're right. I will try to do better." Deep down inside, I knew that I wasn't going to do any better. I blamed Reagan for what happened to Logan. My best friend had been missing for months, and now, Reagan's best friend was not only here, but he was getting to do with her what I couldn't do with Logan. Reagan had the thing I wanted most, senior year with his best friend.

As we walked back inside, I tried my best to fake a smile, but I wasn't happy, and by the look on her face, Cassie clearly wasn't either.

Nevertheless, Reagan was happy, and right now, that was all that mattered.

The next few months were uneventful. There were no more leads as to Logan's whereabouts, and school was virtually drama-free. Reagan and I had been spending more time together which made him happy. I did love him, and a part of me probably always would. However, dating him was not an option now and probably never would be. Logan was missing because he went to bring Reagan home for me. He left for me and was missing because of me. How could I justify dating the person partially responsible for my best friend's abduction? I couldn't and I wouldn't, but every time Reagan and I hung out, I could sense that he was planning to ask me to be his girlfriend. I did my best to ignore it, but I knew it was coming. I just didn't know when.

The school year flew by so quickly. It was already time for homecoming. I knew Reagan was going to ask me, but that was the last thing I wanted. When I got to school, I decided to ask Cody before Reagan could ask me.

"Cody, are you going to homecoming?"

"I was planning to. Why do you ask?"

"Well, I was wondering if you would like to go with me?"

"Riley, are you seriously asking me to homecoming? I'm not saying no, but that just doesn't seem like you."

"I'm not sure what that's supposed to mean, but I'll ask again, and hopefully, you'll say yes this time. Cody, will you…"

"Wait!" Cody interrupted promptly. "I'm the guy. I should be doing the asking, but I want to do it right."

Although I had prompted Cody to ask me, I was still flattered that he wanted to make it special, and I was secretly a little excited to see what he would do.

As I watched Cody walk over to his locker, I noticed Reagan staring at me in the distance. He started walking down the hall towards me. I didn't want him to ask me before Cody had the chance, so I closed my locker, turned my back to him, and walked to class. I heard him yelling my name, but I pretended to be preoccupied. Ignoring Reagan was a daunting task especially when he had his mind set on talking to me. Nevertheless, I was able to avoid him all day until I stopped by my locker to drop off my books. When I closed my locker, there he was grinning from ear to ear.

"Riley, I know that we have been dancing around what we are and what we mean to each other, but I'm ready to put a label on it. Will you do me the honor of being my girlfriend and my date to homecoming?"

He said as he pulled a bouquet from behind his back as well as a box of chocolate.

"I…um…I don't…" I couldn't find the words to respond. I wanted to be with him, and the only reason I wasn't was because of Logan. As I stood there contemplating, I was interrupted by "Oohs" and "Ahhs" coming from behind me. I turned around and saw Cody standing underneath a banner that said "Riley, we are meant to be. Go to homecoming with me."

For a moment, it was like the world had stopped, and I felt horrible. I had convinced Cody to ask me, and now, he had made it clear to the school that he had feelings for me. Reagan laid his heart on the line, but I could not get past the guilt I would feel if I dated him. I decided to go with my gut for once instead of overanalyzing the situation.

"Yes, I will go to homecoming with you, and I will be your girlfriend," I said as I ran to Cody and wrapped my arms around him. I never turned around to see Reagan's reaction. I just heard the sound of the flowers and chocolate hitting the floor.

I didn't want to hurt Reagan, but every time we tried to make things work, something bad ended up happening. I just couldn't take that chance again.

Cody could see that something was bothering me, but he didn't want to ruin the moment. "I'm glad you said yes, Riley."

"So am I."

Chapter Four

Homecoming weekend was finally here! We were all assembled at the pep rally as the spirit squad let us in the school cheer.

"Sing it loud! Say it proud! Moon Ridge Warriors gonna take you down. Victory is ours to gain. Come on, Warriors, let's bring the pain!"

I knew it made me a complete nerd, but pep rallies were the highlight of school for me. I didn't always have the most school spirit, but I was always able to muster up enough for pep rallies and games especially since I was still a cheerleader. I knew it was so cliché that I was a cheerleader dating a jock, but I didn't mind. Being cliché was much better than being alone.

Once school was over, the cheerleaders got ready for the homecoming game. I was excited because I was usually a spotter, or I was on the floor. However, tonight, I was going to be a flyer. I couldn't wait. My family was going to be there, and Cody was actually going to see me cheer. I was a little nervous because we had just started dating, and Reagan was devastated. I wasn't sure how he would handle being on the court with Cody. We needed this win, and I didn't want to be the cause of our team losing.

As time wound down, crowds of people poured into the gym. The boys were introduced over the P.A. Since it was homecoming and a few of the players were seniors, they received special recognition after the team was on the court. Everyone applauded as the seniors' names rang out over the loudspeaker.

"And now presenting, Reagan Alexander, Gabriel Cole, Jadon Cole, and Cody Hale"

The applause was so loud that my ears were ringing, but I didn't mind because this was our night and our time to shine.

Coach Thomas hushed the crowd after several minutes of cheers and applause.

"Everyone, please, may I have a moment to speak."

The crowd grew silent and took their seats.

"Thank you," he paused and cleared his throat. "As most of you know, there is one other senior who is not with us tonight. That senior is Logan Andrews. While he might not be here with us physically, he is definitely here in spirit. Whether you know him or you don't, please stand and join me in a moment of silence followed by a round of applause."

Everyone, young and old, did as he said, and for that moment, it really did feel as though

Logan was there. Still, as beautiful as the moment was, we had a game to play. This was not just any game; we were playing against our archrivals the Coral Springs Hound Dogs. They had been training all year for this game, but so had we.

Although every game mattered, certain games meant more to us, our school, and our community. With all of the crime and people turning up missing, our town needed hope, and that's exactly what the basketball team intended to give.

The referee threw the ball up in the air, and with that, the biggest game of the season began. CSHS gained possession of the ball first, but that didn't last for long. Cody intercepted a pass and took the ball down the court for an easy layup. From then until halftime, the score remained close.

The boys followed Coach Thomas into the locker room as the halftime show began. Our cheerleading squad had come in 2nd place at Sectionals last year, and we still didn't perform the way we did at halftime. I loved the rush of being thrown into the air knowing that I was not going to fall, but the memory of performing so well that the CSHS cheerleaders didn't even do a routine was the highlight of my night.

After we finished our routine, the commentator announced the seniors on the squad.

"And now presenting, Riley Abernathy, Paisley Moore, and Brie West."

We received our applause, and we waited for the homecoming court to be announced. No one knew who would be king and queen. That would be announced at the dance, but the princes and princesses would be announced.

"As I call your names, please meet at the red carpet and walk down to receive your sashes and crowns. Here are our princes and princesses: ninth grade, Connor Lee and Rachel Snow; tenth grade, Jeffrey Baker and Anita Wilson; eleventh grade, Dean Taylor and Jenna Law, and our king and queen will be announced at homecoming tomorrow." Miss Rodriguez said with a sparkle in her eye. She had planned homecoming, and she had no intention of letting anyone else do any aspect of her job.

Halftime was finally over, and the third quarter had begun. Both teams came out playing hard. By mid-fourth quarter, the score was tied, but CSHS had gained the lead with 30 seconds left on the clock. Gabe fouled their worst free-throw shooter. He had not made a single free throw all game. He stepped to the line and missed his first shot, but he made the second shot. CSHS was now leading by three with only seven seconds remaining. They ran a full-court press against us. Nevertheless, this was what the team had prepared for over the last two months. Jadon threw the ball in; Reagan found an opening and passed the ball down the court to Cody. With two seconds left, Cody threw the ball up in the air from behind the arc. As he did, he was knocked to the ground by the other team. The ball bounced off the backboard and continued to bounce around the rim until it went through the net. The game was tied, and Cody had a free throw to shoot. He was the best free-throw shooter on the team, but his wrist had gotten injured. He could not take the shot. With all of the starters on the court,

Coach Thomas was forced to put in a player from the bench.

"Wesley James, you're in."

Wes was in shock. He started walking out on the court, but Coach Thomas pulled him back.

"Listen, kid, you need to block everyone and everything out or you will miss. Just focus on the thing that makes you happiest and shoot the ball."

Wes ran to the free-throw line. He set his feet, took a deep breath, and shot the ball. We all expected him to miss, so we started gathering our belongings before he had shot. Some people had walked out of the gym already, but the sound of the ball touching the net got our attention. Wes made the shot and won the game for us.

Every MRV fan in the stands cheered because we had finally won a homecoming game. The basketball team and the cheer squad wanted to go out and celebrate after the game, but homecoming was the next day.

The next morning, I woke up before my alarm clock rang. When I looked at my phone, Paisley and Brie had already texted me. We were supposed to meet at the mall to get our hair and nails done. However, our appointment time was moved up, so the girls were on their way to get me. I hopped out of bed and jumped in the shower. Ten minutes later, I ran downstairs, grabbed a pop tart, and ran out of the door. The girls were already waiting for me when I got outside.

"Come on, Riley. Hop in, we have tons to do, and barely any time to do it." Paisley yelled out of the window.

"Ok, ok, I'm coming." I said out of breath as I slammed the front door. I went to open the back door of the car, but I stopped myself when I saw a figure moving in the backseat. Paisley was driving, and Brie was riding shotgun. I had no idea who could be in the backseat. Still, I had a bad feeling in the pit of my stomach.

"Riley, get in! We're gonna be late." Brie said slightly agitated.

I opened the door and couldn't believe who I saw. I wanted to snap, but I kept my mouth shut.

"Hey, Riley!"

"Hi Cassie, what are you doing here?"

Brie and Paisley repeatedly cleared their throats and were glaring at me in the rearview mirror, but I ignored them and repeated my initial question.

"What are you doing here, Cassie?"

"I'm going to homecoming with you guys. Reagan asked me, and I said yes. The guys all chipped in for the limo, so I'll be here all day and night." Cassie was grinning from ear to ear.

I just wanted to throat punch her. I might be with Cody, but Reagan was still off-limits in my book.

"Why? Why can't I shake Reagan? What is wrong with me?" My mind continued to reel until we pulled into the mall parking lot.

"Cassie, I'm sorry. I'm glad you're here, and I'm glad we all get to hang out. I was shocked, and I reacted inappropriately."

"It's fine, Riley. I know you have feelings for Reagan. I don't know why you let him go, but it's your loss. I don't want any drama, so let's just be friends and move on."

Cassie irked me so much, but she was right. "I let him go, so I have to let him go." That thought hurt me, but it was reality.

We went into the mall and got our hair and nails done. We also picked up our dresses and went to the school to finish the last of the homecoming decorations. Once we finished, Paisley drove us back to her house, so we could get dressed. The limo pulled up at 5:00. Around 5:30, we came downstairs to meet our dates and to get our pictures taken.

As I walked downstairs, I locked eyes with Reagan, and I started to feel flushed. I expected him to be watching Cassie, but he was watching me. "Why was he watching me?" I wasn't the only one who noticed. Cody looked irritated and stepped in front of Reagan to help me down the stairs. However, I knew Cody really stood there so I would lock eyes with him. I felt awful. This was supposed to be a special night for Cody and me, and it already had a rough start. Still, I had every intention of making the night one to remember.

After we put on our corsages, we went outside for pictures. Paisley's mom was a photographer; that was the only reason my mom allowed me to get dressed elsewhere. Mrs. Moore finished our pictures in an hour, and we left for homecoming.

The hotel was spectacular, and the view was amazing. The venue was better than I could have ever imagined. As we walked in under the shimmering lights, I felt something that I hadn't felt in a long time, happiness.

Chapter Five

Cody was the perfect gentleman all night. From pulling out my chair and holding the door to getting my drinks, he made sure to cover all of the bases. It was almost like he was reading my mind. We danced the night away, and for the first time in a long time, Reagan and Logan were the last things on my mind.

"Riley, are you having a good time?" Cody asked timidly.

"I am. I definitely am. Are you?" The uncertainty in his voice made me wonder if he was enjoying himself as much as I was.

"The dance is all right. Being here with you is the best part."

He seemed to know just what to say to make me blush.

After a few more dances, we went to get our pictures taken in the photobooth. Then, we gathered in the middle of the dance floor for the announcement of the homecoming king and queen. The DJ started playing quiet but suspenseful music just before Miss Rodriguez stepped in front of the mic. I couldn't help but laugh because it was all so dramatic for something as trivial as homecoming.

Until the announcement, no one knew who had been nominated.

"For homecoming king, the nominees are Reagan Alexander, Cody Hale, and Zander West."

I couldn't believe Cody had been nominated when this was his first year at Moon Ridge High. He was on stage grinning from ear to ear. His excitement made me laugh.

"For homecoming queen, the nominees are Riley Abernathy, Paisley Moore, and Brie West."

As we waited for Miss Rodriguez to announce the winners, I daydreamed about Cody and me dancing under the spotlight in front of everyone. It would be the perfect end to the perfect night.

"And now, for homecoming king, Reagan Alexander."

Immediately, I knew my dream night was over, but what made it worse was the fact that Cody had to watch Reagan spin me around the dance floor. I felt horrible but amazing at the same time. Being close to Reagan always brought back feelings; still, I did my best to keep my poker face on because I did not want to upset Cody.

Reagan, however, did not care. He was grinning from ear to ear as he spun me around the floor. I knew Cassie was fuming. There was no way anyone could be truly happy as a second pick. At least I know I wouldn't be. I was so preoccupied with my thoughts that I didn't realize the song had ended. Reagan did, but he didn't care. He made sure to take advantage of every second he could. When I finally came back to reality, I realized Cody was gone. I couldn't believe he left me at homecoming by myself. Although I knew it was partially my fault, I still blamed Reagan.

"If you were my date to homecoming, I would never leave you standing in the middle of the dance floor." Reagan said with a devious smirk on his face.

It was moments like this that I truly felt as close to hate as I could without actually hating him. I rolled my eyes and walked around the hall to look for Cody. After twenty minutes, my feet started to hurt, and I just wanted to go home. I took off my shoes and walked outside. It was a nice night, so I decided to walk home to clear my head.

I walked for what felt like hours. My legs were going numb, and I had to rest. I found a park bench and sat awaiting the Destination Now driver. Before I knew it, I had fallen asleep. The next morning, I woke up in my bed with no recollection of what had happened the night before.

I was a little groggy when I got out of bed. looked in the mirror and saw that I had a few bruises on my face, but I had no idea how I had gotten them. I looked around my room for my phone, but I couldn't find it. I walked downstairs to ask my parents if they had seen it. When I reached the end of the stairs, I found Sheriff Franklin talking to my parents.

"Good morning, Riley." He said with a grim look on his face.

"Good morning, Sheriff. Is everything all right?"

"No Riley, please have a seat."

"Did something happen with Logan?"

"No, do you remember what happened last night after you left the dance?"

"Honestly? No, I remember sitting on a park bench waiting for the Destination Now driver, but I think I dozed off. The next thing I remember was waking up in my bed."

"That's what I was afraid of. Riley, last night you were assaulted while you were sleeping on the bench. The assailant was unable to get very far in his attempts to take advantage of you. Reagan stopped the assailant before things escalated. I know this has been hard for you to hear, but both Reagan and the cameras nearby were able to get a partial image of the assailant. He is in custody right now and will not be released for quite some time."

"Who was it?"

"Cody."

"Cody, are you sure it was Cody? Sheriff, you said that Reagan identified Cody?"

"Yes Riley, remember I also said that the cameras nearby got footage of the assailant. We reviewed them multiple times. Either it was Cody, or someone else looks just like him." Sheriff Franklin replied.

"Sheriff if you don't mind may I please see the footage?" Riley asked timidly.

"Typically, that's not working, and it goes against protocol. However, since you seem certain that it couldn't have been Cody, I will let you view the video. Meet me at the station as soon as you can. Thank you, I apologize for the circumstances of the visit, but I hope you all have a great rest of your day."

As the sheriff walked out of the door, my parents both came over and comforted me knowing that I was extremely shaken up by what had happened.

"Riley, I know you said it can't be Cody, but if it is what are you going to do?"

"I'm not sure dad. I feel like I keep getting myself into situations that I can't get out of, and I'm tired of it. I wish I could go back to my freshman year when my only friend was Logan. Things were so much simpler then. I really miss those days."

My parents hugged me tighter and comforted me saying everything would be ok.

I was still worn out from homecoming night. I decided to take a nap before going to the police station. As I laid in my bed, my mind was reeling. I had made some major mistakes in the past, but this was different. I didn't mean to get myself into these situations. I always pushed people away; it just happened whether I wanted it to or not. Life without Logan had been lonely. It didn't matter how many people were around or how much fun I was having. There was still a hollow feeling in my heart that I could not shake. Homecoming was supposed to be one of the highlights of high school. I had imagined it ever since my first day of freshman year. Logan and I would go shopping together for my dress and heels, and we would pick out his tux. He would bring me an artificial corsage that I would keep for the rest of my life. He would arrive early and would nervously pace back and forth outside before knocking on the door. My parents would answer the door and tell him to wait for me by the staircase. When I made it to the top of the stairs, Logan's mouth would drop because he did not expect me to be made over completely. We would have the best night of our lives. That was what I wanted, but I would have been happy if Logan was wearing sweaty gym clothes and hadn't showered in a week. We had been through so much together. We had so much more to go through together. In that moment, everything finally made sense.

Cody was fun, but he would never fill the void in my heart. Reagan was the boy next door, mysterious and captivating but trouble, nonetheless. Logan was the only one who knew and understood me. He would take on the world for me just to keep the smile on my face. I had wasted so much time trying to find the one who would make me happy. He was in front of me all along, but now, he was gone. I didn't know if he was ever coming back, and I didn't know what I would do if I never saw him again.

Instantly, I woke up violently dripping with sweat and realized I had overslept. I got dressed and rushed to the police station. share Franklin took me in a room so I can view the video. The guy in the video resembled Cody, but I still didn't think it was him. How would Cody have known when I was leaving the dance? He had left long before I did. Why would he try to attack me, especially in a public place, when he knew things were on the rocks with us? It just didn't add up to me. I had already decided not to press charges against Cody because I firmly believed the real perpetrator was still on the loose. Nevertheless, I needed to speak to him first. Officer Franklin walked me to an interrogation room. There sat Cody handcuffed to the chair.

His face looked rather solemn, and he wouldn't make eye contact with me.

"Riley, you only have a few minutes. I'll be waiting on the other side of the door." Sherriff Franklin said as he closed the door behind him.

"So, Cody, do you wanna tell me what happened last night?"

He remained quiet. I could barely hear him breathe.

"Cody, I asked you a question, and I'd really appreciate an answer."

He still said nothing.

"Well, I guess it's safe to say you attacked me then. Enjoy prison."

"Wait, Riley…" Cody said as I walked toward the door.

"I'm listening," I said without turning around.

"I was angry. I went for a walk to clear my head. I didn't realize how far or how long I had walked. On my way back to my car, I saw someone sitting on a bench. Some guy was assaulting a girl on the bench. I hit him over the head with a beer bottle I found on the ground. It got him pretty good, but he still took a swing at me. I fought him off best I could. He ran in the opposite direction. When I turned around, I realized it was you. I panicked and started looking you over to see if he had hurt you. Reagan saw me in the distance and attacked me because he thought I was hurting you. He called the police. They didn't believe my story, and now, here I am."

I walked out of the room without responding. I could hear Cody crying inside the room. I believed his story, and after hearing him out, Sheriff Franklin did as well.

Chapter Six

For the next few weeks, Sheriff Franklin heavily reviewed the footage from the night I was assaulted. There was no clear shot of the assailant's face which made him nearly impossible to identify. The only thing we learned from the footage was the assailant's hair color, blonde.

My parents were determined to catch the man; nonetheless, it seemed clear that no one would be finding the assailant any time soon. I decided not to let it get to me considering his attempt was unsuccessful. Since it was proven that Cody was not guilty, he was finally able to go home, and I could not wait to see him.

The day of Cody's release was one of the happiest days I had experienced in a very long time. I knew he wasn't guilty, and now, everyone knew the same. Mr. Andrews went to pick him up while Mrs. Andrews and I prepared for Cody's return. When he arrived at his house and opened the door, he was surprised to find that we had thrown him a welcome home party. Cody seemed excited to see everyone. He proved to be the life of the party. Between his jail stories and jokes about being wrongfully arrested, there was not a dull moment. Once the party was over, a few of us stayed behind to clean. About 20 minutes into cleaning, Reagan asked Cody to step outside. I was nervous because the two of them were never really able to get along. My curiosity got the best of me, so I decided to peer through the window underneath the curtains. I couldn't hear them, and it was too dark to read their lips. However, things appeared to be calm. I went back to cleaning just before they walked through the door.

"Hey Riley, did you get a good view through the curtain?" Reagan said smugly.

I could feel my face turning strawberry red. Cody saw how uncomfortable I was, so he gave me the chance to compose myself.

"Riley, I need your help with something in the other room."

I followed him into the kitchen.

"Thank you, Cody. Reagan is such a jerk sometimes!" I rolled my eyes at the thought of him.

"Yeah, he is, but tonight, he proved to be an ok guy."

"What do you mean?" I looked at him with a hint of intrigue.

He winked at me and said, "You'll see. We might not have worked out, but that doesn't mean you two can't."

As he walked out of the kitchen, he turned and said, "By the way, Reagan apologized for everything, and we're good now."

Cody's homecoming was the push we needed to move forward and to leave the past behind us for good. We were all finally in a good place. Even Cassie and I were getting along. I still missed Logan, but I did not want to be miserable for the rest of my senior year.

The glimmer of hope I once had was fading each day that Logan was gone. I was ready to accept that he was never coming home. Holding on to him had held me back from being happy. I knew there would always be a void in my heart, but trying to move on was a necessity.

As I contemplated what I should do, Cody's words kept playing in my mind.

"You'll see. We might not have worked out, but that doesn't mean you two can't."

It felt like taking a chance on Reagan would be a betrayal of Logan. I just didn't want to forget Logan. I didn't want to leave him behind, but there was no reason for Logan's memory to fade from my mind, especially not after everything we had been through over the years. I wanted to explore things with Reagan, but I would never have been bold enough to tell him that.

One Friday night, a few of us decided to meet at Moon Ridge Lake for a bonfire. We knew our lives would be changing in a couple of months, and we didn't want to miss out on spending time together.

"Hey guys, I have something to say." Reagan cleared his throat. "When I first moved here, I hated everyone and everything. I didn't want to be here, but after getting to know all of you, I don't want to leave. It's been a crazy ride, but I don't regret one moment of it."

"I agree with Reagan. I came here to find my cousin, and that didn't work out. Nevertheless, I found something to keep me going. You guys have been there for me since day one. Things were rocky for a while, but we made it through, and I'm grateful for that. I'm grateful for all of you." Cody raised his cup, and we did too.

I decided to go for a walk down the pier to clear my head. The night was beautiful, and I normally did my best thinking under the stars. As I looked at the water from the edge of the pier, I took a deep breath. Before I could relax and enjoy myself, Zander came running down the pier.

"Hey Riley, are you ok?"

"Yeah, I am. Thanks for checking on me." I tried to hide my annoyance.

"No, you're not. Something has been off with you for months, and you never want to talk about it. If you don't confide in someone soon, you're gonna explode."

"Zander, I appreciate your concern, but you need to go. I am not in the mood to talk, and right now, you're making things worse."

"All right, well, I'm gonna leave you alone. If you need to talk, I'll be by the fire." Zander turned around and walked away.

I sighed and did what I could to clear my head. Watching the waves was one of the things I enjoyed most, but it wasn't bringing me the happiness for which I had hoped.

All I wanted was to be happy, but no matter how hard I tried, I just couldn't be. A feeling of loneliness followed me everywhere I went. As tears began to fill my eyes, I felt someone's arms wrap around me, and I knew who it was as soon as I smelled his cologne.

"Riley, we've been through more than most. Even though things are nowhere near perfect and have grown more complicated over time, I want to be with you. Everything else in my life has fallen into place. I have my family back. My best friend lives here now, but the only thing missing is having you by my side. You don't have to say anything right now. I'm gonna go, so you can think."

He let me go and turned to walk away, but I grabbed his arm before he could. I needed to tell him how I felt because Reagan's words made me feel something I hadn't in a very long time…happiness.

Chapter Seven

A few nights later, I had my first official date with my new boyfriend. Reagan and I had spent time together on many occasions, but being an actual couple made everything feel new, exciting, and a little strange. I wasn't sure what I should wear because I didn't know where we were going. After much deliberation, I decided to wear a sundress and sandals. I rushed downstairs as soon as I heard a knock on the front door. I knew my dad would give Reagan the 3rd degree if I didn't get to the door first. Nonetheless, I tripped and fell down the stairs as my dad opened the door. My mom was walking past and somehow managed to break my fall with neither of us getting hurt. I would have been so embarrassed if it were anyone else who had seen me fall. However, it was Reagan. We both laughed, cracked a few jokes, and moved on like nothing had happened. Reagan helped me up off of the floor and handed me the bouquet of roses he was holding behind his back.

"Thank you, Reagan. They are beautiful."

"Yeah, but you're more beautiful." He said shyly.

My parents were giggling profusely, so I quickly ushered Reagan out of the door.

As Reagan opened the door for me, I felt a chill run down my spine and had an eerie feeling that someone was watching me.

"Riley, is everything ok?"

"Everything is perfect."

We went to a fancy new restaurant downtown in the valley. I couldn't believe how expensive the food was. I was afraid to order anything but a glass of water. Reagan could see that the prices had me on edge.

"Riley, we can go somewhere else if you want to, but you don't have to worry about the price if we stay here."

"I appreciate you trying to impress me, but I'm pretty easy going. We can go somewhere else if you don't mind."

"I don't mind at all. I wanted to take you somewhere nice, but I'll have a good time with you no matter where we are." He said as he winked at me.

We left the restaurant and went for a walk on the strip. Reagan noticed a food truck called Kebabin' Rob. As soon as I saw the name, I wanted to try the food just as badly as Reagan. I ordered a kebabwich, and he ordered a kebaco supreme. The food was great as was the atmosphere. Rob had rented the space for his truck, and he also had a portable dance floor set up next to the truck. A live band was playing, and I felt like dancing. I dragged Reagan onto the dance floor. He whispered something to me, but I couldn't hear him. The music was so loud, I couldn't even hear myself think.

Reagan repeated himself, "I can't dance."

I still couldn't hear him. "What did you say?"

"I can't dance!" He yelled just as the music stopped.

I knew he was embarrassed so I replied, "I can't either! That's why this is so fun!"

The two of us twirled around the dance floor and looked awful doing it. Our go-to dance moves were the sprinkler, the towel, and the lawnmower, and we made them look good.

Time passed by so quickly. When I checked my phone, I realized that I had 20 minutes to get home. We ran back to the car and rushed down the road. I'll never understand how Reagan made a 30-minute trip take 15 minutes, but we made it just in time to see my parents peering through the curtains. My dad opened the door as soon as he saw Reagan get out of the car.

"Goodnight, Reagan," My dad said sternly.

"Goodnight, sir," Reagan replied as he opened my car door, hugged me, and walked home.

"You were cuttin' it pretty close to your curfew, baby girl."

"I know, Dad; I'm sorry. We lost track of time. Have a good night."

"Sleep well, baby girl."

As I went upstairs, I could feel my phone vibrating. It was Reagan.

"Hello," I whispered.

"Hey Riley, I just called to say goodnight, and I had a great time."

"Goodnight Reagan, I did too."

I went to bed with the biggest smile on my face that night, and thanks to Reagan, that smile was continually on my face night after night.

Things with Reagan were going surprisingly well. He had proven to be the perfect gentleman. Reagan opened and closed every door for me. He paid for every date even when I offered to chip in. He took the time to plan our dates and always found a way to make me feel special. Before I realized it,

Reagan had filled the void in my heart where Logan used to be.

Everyone was happy to see me happy, and I was happy to see them moving on and finding happiness of their own. Because our group spent so much time together, we became like one big family. With the exception of Zander, everyone was coupled up. Cody and Cassie had grown very close over time and had finally started dating. They had a lot in common and actually made a very cute couple. Omar and Brie were able to figure out how to overcome the countless challenges they had faced ever since the beginning of their relationship. It was great to see them smiling instead of arguing and laughing instead of crying. Nevertheless, Zander was alone. Although he would never admit it, I knew he felt lonely, and I knew he wanted to find his person. Secretly, I always thought that Zander and Paisley would be a great match, but Paisley was in a long-term relationship until two weeks ago. Gabe had graduated early and was moving to Texas for college. Since he was eligible for early admission, he was going to be leaving Moon Ridge Valley two days after graduation. Paisley had been accepted to NYU, and she was not leaving until mid-August. Gabe knew that the long-distance would put a lot of strain on their relationship. He wanted Paisley to have a chance at a fresh start. Gabe broke up with her one week before their four-year anniversary. Though Paisley was devastated, she knew that Gabe's decision was best for both of them. They vowed to remain friends and did not close the door on reuniting in the future. Since Paisley had just come out of a serious relationship, I did not want to push Zander on her. Still, I thought Zander and Paisley could be very happy together.

The next time our group went out, I invited Paisley to tag along so she could have something to do other than wallowing. I didn't expect Paisley to say yes, but she did. While I was not trying to set them up, I was ok if they ended up together. We went to see the newly released vampire movie *Fangs & Freedom*.

Whether intentionally or by mistake, Zander and Paisley ended up sitting next to each other. Zander kept mumbling things under his breath, and Paisley couldn't help but laugh. It was nice to see her smiling again. Although I wanted to see how things were progressing, I needed to stop being nosy so I could focus on Reagan. The movie was better than we thought it would be. We all had a great time.

Once it was time to leave, Reagan let me know that he had a surprise for me, but we would have to go somewhere to get it. I was so excited. As we were getting into the car to leave, Paisley walked over to my door.

"Hey, Paisley, what's up?"

"Not much, I was just wondering if I can sleep over at your house tonight. I really need to talk to you."

I did my best to hide my disappointment. "Of course, you can!" I knew Reagan was probably upset with me, but Paisley needed me.

"I'm sorry." I whispered to Reagan before Paisley got in the car.

Reagan did his best to keep a smile on his face.

"So Paisley, what did you think of the movie?" Reagan asked trying to stifle his frustration.

"It was good. I didn't think I would have as much fun as I did." She replied.

He knew she had been miserable post break up. "That's great, Paisley. I'm really glad you had a good time. I watched his heart melt and his expression change. I knew he was a big softy.

The rest of the ride was pretty quiet. Paisley spent most of the time staring out of the window. I could tell she had a lot on her mind.

When we got to my house, I hugged Reagan, said goodbye, and hurried inside with Paisley.

I had messaged my parents to let them know that Paisley was coming over. They went to the store and picked up a Girls Night in Breakup Kit.

Paisley and I went upstairs to my room. We opened the GNI Kit, sat on the bed, and started chatting.

"So Riley, there's something I need to tell you."

"Ok, what is it?"

"I think I have feelings for Reagan."

My face turned ghostly white as I contemplated what to say.

"Are you…?" Paisley immediately interrupted me.

"I'm just kidding, but I do have a crush. I just feel like it might be too soon to date."

"A crush? On whom?" I was praying she would say anyone but Reagan. Otherwise, we would have a serious problem,

"I always thought Zander was cute, but I would never have pursued him. Gabe was my everything. I thought we were endgame like you and Reagan."

"So, are you planning to pursue Zander now?"

"Honestly, I don't know. I heard he is going to Columbia University, so we won't be that far away from each other once we leave Moon Ridge."

"Well, it sounds like you have some things to figure out."

"I guess. I won't chase after him though. Still, if he asks me out, I'm not saying no."

I could tell Paisley felt better after getting everything off her chest.

"Paisley, I have a secret that I haven't told anyone, but I need to tell someone."

"Ok…"

"Promise me you will not repeat this to anyone."

"I won't. I promise."

"No, promise me on your extensions."

"But Riley, these extensions cost $500."

"Exactly."

"Ok, I promise on my extensions. So, what is the big secret."

"I'm pretty sure someone has been following me. I keep feeling like I am being watched, but the first time Reagan took me out a few weeks ago, I am positive someone was watching me."

"What? When did you start sensing that someone was following you?"

"A few days after the attack on prom night."

"Riley, are you serious?"

"I know I should have told someone sooner, but I don't think it's the same person who attacked me."

"Attacker or not, with all the psychopaths running around shooting and abducting people, I would expect you to be a little smarter. I mean, how many times do people have to try to kill you before you wake up?"

"Paisley, I know you think I'm an idiot, but this is my story to tell. My secret is now yours to keep. If I feel like I'm in any danger, I will call Sheriff Franklin. I promise."

I knew Paisley still wasn't convinced, but tonight was supposed to be about her. I rifled through the kit and pulled out a movie. The rest of the night we relaxed, ate snacks, and watched movies. Although the night started off rocky, we ended up having a lot of fun.

In the morning, before Paisley left, she warned me to be careful and to reconsider keeping my secret a secret. I knew she was right, but I had no proof that I was being followed. Moreover, I did not want to worry anyone needlessly.

Chapter Eight

Time had flown by so quickly. Our last days at Moon Ridge Valley High were coming to an end. With finals, SATs, and graduation on our minds, we were too busy to do anything but study. Because we were under a lot of stress and didn't have much time to spend together, we decided to meet for a study session at Comela. Many of our other classmates were there studying as well. Before we arrived, I called the manager, Ricardo, and asked him if he could host an exam trivia session for us. He agreed, but we had to come in after the dinner rush. Ricardo let us study from 9-12.

Around 10:15, one of the waitresses handed me a note. It read, "How could you do this to me? Betrayal does not look good on you."

I looked around for the waitress, but I couldn't find her. I asked everyone on the waitstaff. I didn't recognize her, and I was a regular at Comela. I ended up bumping into a waiter on his way to the kitchen. He let me know that she was new and that she had stepped outside for a moment.

He also said, "She disappears a lot. It's kinda weird, and she's probably gonna get fired soon. If you know her, tell her to get her stuff together."

"Thank you," I said before going outside.

By the time I found out where she had gone, I couldn't find her anywhere. Nonetheless, I still had an eerie feeling of being watched. I knew she wasn't the one who wrote the note. As I continued to look around, panic set in. Everything was spinning, and I felt like I was going to pass out.

Reagan came running outside with a brown paper bag. He knew something was wrong when he didn't see me return for a while. He went searching for me and saw me outside. He had been watching me from the window. I didn't know at the time, but Paisley had broken her promise to me. After the sleepover, she stopped by Reagan's house and told him about my potential stalker. Reagan had been watching out for me ever since.

I breathed into the bag for a few minutes before feeling better.

"Riley, what's going on? Why are you out here?"

"I was looking for someone, but she's gone now."

"Who is she? Are you doing ok?"

"No, I'm not." I slipped the note into his hand and sat down on the bench in front of the restaurant.

As he read the note, I could see a look of fear, panic, and anger on his face. "Who gave this to you, Riley?"

"A waitress," I said on the verge of tears.

"So, someone has been following you, you've kept it a secret, and now, you're receiving ominous notes?"

"Wait, how did you…?" Reagan interrupted me.

"You already know how I found out, but that is irrelevant. We don't know who sent you this or who has been watching you. There are far too many unaccounted-for people with grudges against you. I don't care what you say; I am talking to Sheriff Franklin immediately. Go back inside. I'll be in once I get off of the phone."

I composed myself and walked inside. Although I was upset with Paisley for breaking her promise, I was grateful that Reagan knew. He was always ready and willing to do the things I couldn't.

I sat back down at the table and acted as if nothing had happened. Fifteen minutes later, we were startled by the screams of a woman.

"Help, help! Somebody call 911!" She yelled piercingly.

I rushed outside to see who needed help and where Reagan was. When I stepped through the door, I heard a light splash as my feet hit the ground. I almost slipped and fell. Immediately, I looked down and let out a blood-curdling scream.

"Reagan! Help! Help! Someone help!" I didn't know how long Reagan had been lying on the ground, but I knew he had lost a lot of blood. By the time he was found, he had passed out. There were no witnesses; however, there was a note on the knife that stabbed him.

"Riley, this is your fault. You did this to Reagan. Say goodbye to him, or I will kill him."

"Everyone, back up! Move away from the body." The EMT yelled.

Although I heard him, I didn't process what he had said.

Moments later, I was being dragged off of Reagan kicking and screaming. "Let me go! Let go of me! Stop! Put me down! I need to go to the hospital with him! I said let me go!"

"Put her down now." I heard a familiar voice say. "Put her down, Luke."

"Yes sir, Sheriff Franklin. "He put me down and went to help the other EMTs life Reagan on to the stretcher.

"Riley, I'll give you a ride to the hospital. I think there are some things we need to talk about."

I knew I had a lot of explaining to do; I also knew this never would have happened if I had said something sooner.

"Riley, Reagan was on the phone with me when this happened. I heard a lot of background noise as the phone fell. The call became muffled. The last thing I heard him say was, 'You don't have to do this. Why are you doing this?'"

"Are you saying it's someone we know?"

"No, I'm saying it's someone Reagan knows, and once he wakes up, he can tell us."

"Did Reagan tell you anything when he called?"

"He told me about your stalker. I believe the stalker might be your attacker. I also think it could be the same person who attacked Reagan."

When we pulled in front of the hospital, I handed Sheriff Franklin both notes. I told him about the waitress handing me one. I also told him that I had removed the other note from the knife.

While I knew that tampering with evidence was a crime, I also knew that note would have been illegible after being drenched with Reagan's blood.

"Thank you for the ride, Sheriff. I will keep you updated."

"Good, one of my officers will drive you home. You, your house, and your family are under 24/7 surveillance until this case is solved."

He went back to Comela to get some information from Ricardo while I went inside to see how Reagan was doing.

I sat in the waiting room with Reagan's family. I thought they knew what had happened to him, but they didn't. They had so many questions. I felt beyond overwhelmed.

"Riley, what happened?" We got a phone call saying Reagan was in the hospital. Miss Rachel said panicking.

"He was stabbed."

"Stabbed? Who stabbed him?" Mr. Alexander asked.

"I don't know, but I wish I did."

"Riley, how did this happen? I thought you all were studying." Miss Rachel seemed more hostile than sad.

"We were studying."

"Then, how did he get stabbed, Riley?" Mr. Alexander asked sternly.

"We were studying, but I went outside. He followed me."

"Riley, did you stab him?"

"No, I would never. I love him."

"If you really love him, tell us what happened! We are his parents, and we need answers."

"Ok, ok, someone has been stalking me. Reagan found out about it and has been watching over me. I went outside because I got a creepy note. It was probably from the stalked. Reagan followed me outside. I told him about the note, and he told me to go back inside while he spoke to Sheriff Franklin. He was stabbed after I went inside. The knife had a note on it which I gave to the Sheriff. I…"

I was interrupted by Miss Rachel's hand across my face. I was in complete shock. I couldn't believe she slapped me.

"Riley, you will stay away from my son. You will never go near my son again. Being with you and loving you are the reasons he is hurt once again. You are poison to everyone around you. because being with you is a death sentence. I will not lose him because of you."

Before she could regret what she had said, I went running out of the hospital.

Ms. Grady had returned from the restroom just in time to hear the latter portion of her daughter's life-altering words.

"Rachel, you should be ashamed of yourself. That girl is one of the best things ever to come into his life. When he wakes up and finds out what you've done, he will never forgive you." Ms. Grady didn't wait for a response. She chased after me as I was getting into the deputy's car.

It was then that my phone began to ring. Sheriff Franklin was on the other end of the line.

"Riley, are you still with Reagan's family?" He asked.

"Yes, Ms. Grady is standing here with me."

"All right, listen very closely and do as I say. I think I know who is following you. I also think I know who attacked you. Still, I need to be sure. What did the waitress with the note look like?"

"She had black and purple hair and was lightly tanned. She was wearing glasses and a headband."

"Ok, thank you. Go home with Ms. Grady. I have a deputy waiting in front of her house. After the last incident, we put cameras around her home. Your stalker wouldn't know that, so meet with my deputy for further instruction."

After I hung up with him, Ms. Grady and I got into the police car.

When we arrived, an unmarked vehicle was in Ms. Grady's drive.

"Hello, I am Deputy Pete. I have something I need you to review."

We went inside and watched footage on his laptop. He flipped through clip after clip of the footage, but we didn't see anything. He decided to search the dates a few days before my attack. Ms. Grady asked him to pause the recording because she saw a blurry figure in the bushes. The image was very poor, but we both saw a blonde male with glasses and a beard standing in the bushes in front of my house. It was too hard to tell if he was my attacker, but he did show up in the footage several times upwards to and before the attack. The deputy went back to the station to run facial recognition on the image, and I went home.

My parents knew I had had a rough day, so they gave me some space to clear my head. That night I cried myself to sleep.

Chapter Nine

While Ms. Grady and I were with the deputy, Sheriff Franklin was investigating the crime scene. He decided to speak to the manager about the waitress.

"Ricardo, tonight a purple-haired waitress was at your restaurant. I heard she is new. What's her name?"

"Ivy Mae."

"Do you have a copy of her license and her current address?"

"Yes sir," Ricardo want to the back room and returned with her file. "Here it is."

As Sheriff Franklin looked through her file, all he could do was shake his head. "Did you even look at her information?"

"Of course, I did. She seemed a little off, but she's from out of town, so I didn't question her information."

"All right, consider this a teachable moment and a friendly warning. This ID is fake. It's a good fake, but there are obvious tells if you know what you're looking for. Look at her name. Who is named Ivy Mae Mae? Also, this can't be a real address. 1234 Furry Beetlewing BN? What is BN? Barn? Also, WZ is not a state abbreviation. Do you know where she is living now?"

"I don't, but I've seen her leave with a guy who used to be a regular. His name is something artsy sounding like River, Lake, or Snow?"

"Could his name be Rayne?"

"Yeah, that's it. Someone approached him a few days ago and called him Rayne, but he insisted his name was Dilbert. He disappeared shortly after."

"Ok, thank you." Sheriff Franklin put out an APB on Rayne as soon as he made it to his car. He requested back up and drove to Rayne's last known address.

The deputy who was dispatched to guard Reagan's room went rushing toward the hospital exit when he was stopped by Reagan's parents.

"Where are you going? You're supposed to keep Reagan safe."

"The Sheriff requested back up. I have no time to explain, but I will be back ma'am." He ran through the door and disappeared into the night.

"Zach, I can't believe they are leaving our boy unprotected."

"Rachel, right now, the only thing he needs protection from is you."

"How can you say that to me?"

"You just broke up with his girlfriend for him and pushed her out of his life. What do you plan on telling him when he wakes up looking for Riley?"

"I'll tell him what he needs to hear. Honestly, all he needs to know is she chose not to be there for him because she had better things to do. That should be enough to make him think twice about wanting her around."

"But that's not true, Rachel. You need to fix this, or you will lose him. You will lose both of us." He said as he pulled away from her.

The next morning, I woke up with a hollow feeling in my chest. Miss Rachel's words cut far deeper than a knife ever could, but I knew she was right. I didn't want to do anything but lay in bed all day, and that's what I intended to do. I rolled over to grab my phone and realized I had eight new voicemails. Both Sheriff Franklin and Mr. Alexander had called me.

I was hesitant to listen to all of the voicemails, but I knew I had no other choice.

Reagan's dad had called to apologize for his wife's behavior. He also let me know what she was planning. He told me to come to the hospital as soon as I woke up, so I did.

On the way, I listened to the voicemails Sheriff Franklin left. He gave me a summary of what happened at Comela when he spoke to Ricardo. Sheriff Franklin also told me to be vigilant. He was supposed to call me back at 7:00, but it was almost 10:00. By the time I arrived at the hospital, the lots were already full. I had to ride the shuttle to the E.R. entrance; I spotted Miss Rachel walking through the lot. Thankfully she didn't see me. However, Reagan's dad did; he took her to a different hospital entrance. I knew I only had a few minutes to see Reagan, so I wanted to make them count. When I made it to his room, he was still recovering. Ms. Grady had been sitting with him all morning, but she left the room and stood watch because Miss Rachel would be arriving soon.

I wasn't sure if Reagan could hear me or not, but I spoke to him as if he did.

"Hey you, I can't stay long, but I have to tell you something. I have to stay away from you. Your mom made that very clear. Being in my life just brings you pain and gets you hurt. I love too much to let anything else happen to you."

Reagan did not wake up or respond, but I did see a single tear roll down his cheek.

"Goodbye Reagan," I said as I walked out of his room. I hurried down the hall and ran through the glass doors, never looking back.

When I made it to my car, there was a note on my windshield. I looked around the lot, but I didn't see anyone.

The note said, "You made the right choice, Riley."

I had grown so weary of these games being played. I just wanted my attacker to be caught, and I wanted things to go back to normal. As I drove through the lot, someone darted out in front of me. It was a male with blonde hair, a beard, and sunglasses. Although I couldn't be sure, he looked a lot like the blurry image I had seen on the deputy's screen. He ran and jumped into a car with the purple-haired waitress. I couldn't be sure who it was, but there was someone else in the vehicle.

"Ring, ring, ring," I picked up my phone and saw that Sheriff Franklin was calling.

"Hi Sheriff, I was just about to call you. What is going on?"

"No one was home when we arrived at Rayne's house, but we found evidence that someone was being kept in their basement. The forensic team is checking the evidence we found for DNA. When were you going to call me?"

"When I came out of the hospital, there was a note on my car. I didn't see anyone in the lot, so I got in my car and started driving. Some guy ran out in front of me. He looked like the guy in the surveillance footage."

"Where is he now, Riley?"

"He got into a car with the purple-haired waitress, and she pulled out as soon as he did."

"What direction are they heading?"

"We are going north on Ridgeline Blvd."

"Do not follow them, Riley. Head to the police station to give a description of the car and the people in it."

"I can't Sheriff. They are not getting away. I need this to end right now." I hung up the phone so he wouldn't talk me out of my decision.

I trailed far back so the driver wouldn't notice me. Nonetheless, it seemed that she did. After twenty minutes of twists, turns, and cutting across traffic, I lost her. I pulled my car over, got out, and started screaming. I felt like I was going out of my mind. Once I calmed down, I did what the Sheriff told me to do. I went to the police station and gave a description of the vehicle and the assailants.

A request for back up came through while I was describing the vehicle. Sheriff Franklin was going back to Rayne's house to see if anyone had returned. On the way, he saw the vehicle I had described. He also saw who was sitting in the backseat. It was Rayne.

The driver began to swerve in and out of lanes. Sheriff Franklin could not continue the pursuit due to the hazardous driving conditions for everyone else on the road. As the vehicle slipped off into the distance, another request came through.

I did not know what the sheriff had said, but fifteen officers left their desks and drove off with sirens blazing. Once I finished my description, Deputy Pete asked me to stick around for a moment.

"Riley, we were able to find five potential matches for the male on surveillance. Do you know any of these people?"

My face turned pale as I looked through the images on the computer. I had no idea who the first four people were, and the thought of them stalking me made me sick to my stomach. Just before the last face came on the screen, another deputy came over to pull Deputy Pete to the side. The final image was Logan. I was so confused. Logan wouldn't do something like that, and he definitely would not come back to town and keep his return a secret.

When Deputy Pete returned, he said, "Riley, brace yourself. The DNA results came back with a positive match for..."

"Logan," I said with a grim look on my face.

"How did you know, Riley?"

"Look at your computer screen, sir."

I walked out and called my mom as soon as I got into the car.

"Riley, is everything ok?"

"No Mom, everything is worse than I could have imagined."

"What happened?"

As I explained the situation to my mom, I knew there was nothing she or anyone else could do to make me feel better.

"Riley, if what you have said is true, something had to have happened to him to make him do this. I have to call the Andrews, but I want you to come straight home."

I did as she said. I had no idea how Logan ended up with Rayne, but I knew I wouldn't get answers until the purple-haired girl was caught.

Chapter Ten

Sheriff Franklin returned to the police station after he was informed that Logan had returned to town. He could not understand how this could have happened or why.

"Deputy Pete, was any other DNA found on the rope?"

"We are waiting for the rest of the results, sir."

"All right, keep me informed." Sheriff Franklin said as he walked into his office and closed the door.

Shortly after, he called me once more. "Riley, I'm sure you heard the news about Logan. If there is any chance of us finding him, we need to know who the purple-haired girl is. Is there anything else you can remember about her?"

"I gave my best description to…"

I heard loud banging on the other end of the line.

"The results came in, sir."

"Ok Pete, what were the results?"

"The DNA came back positive for Chloe Jacobs."

"How Pete? How?"

"I called the facility she was admitted to after her bail was posted. They cleared her and sent her home with her family.

"Are you certain, Pete?"

"Yes, I am, sir."

I hung up the phone before Sheriff Franklin came back on the line. I didn't want him to know that I heard everything.

I could not understand how I looked at Chloe but didn't recognize her. It made no sense that she would have Logan with her for all this time. He was behaving erratically, and I knew Chloe was to blame. I had pulled up in front of my house while my mom was explaining things to Mrs. Andrews. I waved to her, so she would know I made it home safely. As soon as she turned her back, I slipped out of the door and drove to the hospital. Miss Rachel was heading out of the glass doors while I was walking through them.

"Riley, what are you doing here? You are not going to see Reagan."

I continued walking past her and did not respond. She grabbed my arm and pulled me toward her.

"Little girl, did you hear what I just said? Do not walk away from me."

Hospital security saw what had happened and came over to prevent the situation from escalating.

"Ma'am, you need to let her go, immediately." He said sternly.

Miss Rachel let me go, but she turned around and walked back to Reagan's room.

"Miss, are you ok? Do you need your wrist checked?"

"No sir, but thank you for asking."

I didn't need any more problems, but I had to tell Reagan what was going on.

There was a lot of commotion in the hall. I wasn't sure what was going on, but I noticed that the commotion was growing louder as I got closer to Reagan's room.

As soon as Miss Rachel saw me, she ran toward me. Mr. Alexander grabbed her before she could hit me again. I could tell that he was really embarrassed by her behavior. Security escorted her outside and told her she could not return to the hospital until Reagan's release.

The security guard let me know that I could press charges, but that's not what Reagan needed right now. He had been asleep before the commotion, but he was still groggy and was unaware of what happened.

Reagan's face lit up as I walked into the room.

"Hey babe, long time no see."

I stood there silently staring at him because it felt like he had no idea that we were broken up.

"Riley, why are you standing there like a deer in headlights? Get over here and give me a hug."

I reluctantly walked over and hugged him. "How are you feeling, Reagan? Are they discharging you soon?"

"I'm fine, but you're clearly not. What's going on, and where's my mom?"

"Your mom was forcibly removed by security."

"What? Why?"

"I don't think you need to worry about that right now. We have some bigger issues to worry about."

"Bigger than you breaking up with me because my mom told you to…hmm well, ain't that something." He smirked.

"Oh, you know."

"Yeah, Riley, but I'm not accepting a breakup from my mom. That's ridiculous. So, what is the news?"

"Chloe is back in town. Apparently, she was the purple-haired waitress. The police also found out who stabbed you, but no one knows why he did it." I said remorsefully.

"Yeah, I know Logan stabbed me, but I think something is wrong with him. His eyes were hollow like he was just a shell of a person. Honestly, I don't think he knew what he was doing."

"Well, I'm glad you are better. You healed up just in time for graduation. You just have to pass your finals."

"Have I really been in here that long?" Reagan looked concerned.

"Yeah, you have. Graduation is less than a week away. I don't think anyone has had time to process it with all that's been going on. I will see you later though. I have some things to take care of before my parents get home from work."

I walked out of the hospital feeling much better than when I first walked inside.

As I started getting into my car, a familiar voice startled me.

"Riley, don't turn around, and don't say anything."

I was afraid to move because I wasn't sure what was happening. The person pushed me into the backseat, took my keys, and started driving.

I began screaming and banging on the window, but no one could hear me.

"Riley, it's me. Stop freaking out." He said realizing I was on the floor of the car crying.

"Logan! Why are you doing this? Where are you taking me?"

"We are going to the police station. A lot has happened to me, but I only remember bits and pieces."

"Is that blood on your shirt?"

"Yeah, on my way here, I tripped over a low tree branch and landed on some rocks. I think I might have broken something."

"Logan, we were at the hospital! Why didn't you go get medical treatment?" I said loudly hoping he wouldn't hear me dialing 911.

"I will after I go to the police."

"What happened to you? Why were you stalking me and leaving me creepy notes? Why did you stab Reagan?

"Riley, you sound crazy. I have no idea what you are talking about."

I was so confused. He looked and sounded like he was telling the truth, but how could he have done those things and not remember.

A patrol car pulled over behind us, and moments later, the siren was on. Logan pulled off on the side of the road. I expected him to run, but he just sat there like he was innocent.

"Young man, step out of the car with your hands where I can see them." The officer said.

Logan happily obliged the officer. All he said was, "Riley, follow us to the police station, and please ask my parents to come.

I followed the officer to the police station. Although we were much closer to the station, the Andrews arrive before us.

"Logan, Logan, baby don't say anything until your lawyer gets here." Mrs. Andrews said.

"Buddy, we're here for you. We never stopped looking for you. We never gave up on you." Mr. Andrews said.

Actually, seeing Logan face to face made me sad. He looked very frail. He had a lot of scars and did not look like a high school student anymore.

"Riley! Where are you? I'm scared!" Logan said pitifully.

"I'm right here, Logan. I'm right behind you." I felt horrible for him. He genuinely had no idea what was going on or why he was handcuffed.

Sheriff Franklin took Logan into an interrogation room.

"Mr. and Mrs. Andrews, please follow me down the hall. There is something we need to talk about."

"Sheriff, what is going on?" Mrs. Andrews said nervously.

"Logan is not all right. He is behaving erratically."

"What do you mean, Sheriff? Mr. Andrews asked.

"Logan does not know what he has done. His mind is in a fragile state. I am not sure what will happen once I break the news to him."

"Sheriff, can we be the ones to tell our son, please?" Mrs. Andrews pleaded.

"That's not standard protocol, but nothing has been standard in the situation. I'm not sure how he will respond, so be careful. His memories are very real to him even if they are not real to us."

The Andrews were solemn as they walked past us. Mrs. Andrews took my hand and brought me into the room with them. When we walked in, Logan was crying. Being handcuffed to the table was causing him to panic.

"Mom, Dad, why are they treating me like a criminal? I didn't do anything wrong."

Mrs. Andrews began to cry hysterically. She could barely say a word.

Mr. Andrews looked at Logan and said, "Son, your mother and I have something to tell you."

"Dad, what is it? Why is mom crying?"

Mr. Andrews took a deep breath. "Logan, you have been missing for about a year now. During that time, you did some things that were out of character. The police have handcuffed you because you stabbed someone and because you were stalking Riley."

Logan began to laugh.

"Son, this isn't funny. This is serious." Mr. Andrew's heart was breaking with every moment.

Logan continued to laugh.

"Logan, what is so funny?" Mrs. Andrews asked through the tears.

"Why would I stalk my girlfriend? That is ridiculous."

"Son, who is your girlfriend?"

"Dad, come on. It is obviously Riley."

"Logan, you're not da…" I quickly interrupted Mrs. Andrews.

"That's why I came to see you. I wanted to make sure you were ok, Logan."

"So, who did I allegedly stab?"

Sheriff Franklin opened the door before anyone could answer.

"Sorry to interrupt, but I need to speak with Logan."

We all walked into the hall, but we stayed close enough to hear what was going on.

"Logan, why do you think you're here?"

"I came to tell you the location of Smythe, Skye, and Reagan."

"Logan, Skye was brought in about a year ago. She's been serving time ever since. Reagan had also been home for quite some time."

"What do you mean, Sheriff? That doesn't make any sense."

Sheriff Franklin sat back in his chair and stared at Logan momentarily.

"Logan, what is today's date?"

"It's April 24th."

"Of what year?"

"2018 of course," Logan chuckled at the sheriff's trivial questions.

"Logan, it is May 15, 2019."

"But that means I lost a year?"

"Yeah kid, it does, but with a little time, I'm sure you'll get it back."

"So, when you said I stabbed Reagan, that was true?"

"Yes, Logan, this is a serious matter, but you might have some information that will help us both."

"What do you want to know, sir?"

"Where can we find the purple-haired girl?"

Immediately, Logan's eyes glazed over, and he began to yell, "Logan left the basement! Logan is in trouble! Logan needs to go back before they find him!"

"Who are you talking about, Logan? Who is going to find you?"

Logan shut down. I had never seen him look so scared. It made me wonder what had happened to him during that year. Sheriff Franklin left the room as not to agitate Logan any further.

While Sheriff Franklin spoke with the Andrews, I sneaked back into the interrogation room.

"Logan, are you ok?"

"Riley, you came back!"

"Of course, I did. I never left."

Logan started to say something when my phone began to ring.

"Who is that, Riley?"

"No one important." I quickly stuck my phone in my pocket, and as soon as I did, my phone started ringing again.

"Who is calling you, Riley? Tell me now!" He snapped.

I backed away from him slowly and said, "Logan, you are scaring me."

"Riley, who is calling you?" Logan was furious by my lack of response, but I was afraid to answer because I knew exactly who it was.

"Answer me! I said answer me, Riley!"

I remained silent as I turned to open the door.

"It's him, isn't it? What is it gonna take to keep him away from you? I already stabbed him once. Guess, I'll have to do it again."

Sheriff Franklin opened the door and said, "Riley, you need to leave."

"Thank you," I whispered as I rushed through the door. Logan's parents apologized to me. Their apology didn't make me feel any better, but it helped them.

I left the police station knowing that things would never be the same. It was clear that Logan was not entirely lucid. Regardless of what he had said and done, I still loved him the same.

Later that night, I went to see Reagan. He was so excited to be home.

"Hey Reagan, I'm sorry I didn't get here sooner. I spent most of the day at the police station."

"Why? Did something else happen?"

"Yeah, Logan is in holding. If the Sheriff doesn't catch Rayne and Chloe, Logan will go to jail. There is no real explanation for why he is acting the way he is."

"Ok, we will find them. Help me study for my finals, and I will help you catch them.

"This is why I love you, Reagan Grady."

Chapter Eleven

The next morning, Reagan and I woke up with study guides plastered to our faces. We had pulled an all-nighter, but Reagan was wide awake and ready to go. After he went to take his finals, I went back to the police station to check on Logan.

When I arrived, Sheriff Franklin pulled me aside and said, "I'm sorry, Riley, but you can't see Logan today."

"May I ask why?"

"He is a danger to himself and others. We are working on transferring him to somewhere better suited to handle what he is going through."

"Thank you for letting me know."

Just before I walked out, he said, "We will figure out what happened to him. I do not believe that Logan is to blame for any of this, but until we get some answers, Logan will remain in police custody.

Cody stepped through the doors as I was walking out of them.

"Hey Riley, how is Logan doing?"

"I didn't get to see him; he's being transferred elsewhere."

"Why? What did he do?"

"He's still not acting like himself. The police are afraid he might hurt himself or someone else if he remains in holding."

"I know this has got to be hard for him. I don't know what they expect. He's been missing for a year. No one could come back the same after something like that."

"I couldn't agree with you more, but I don't think he'll be in there very long. Reagan and I are going out to look for anything that can help us track Chloe and Rayne down."

"Cassie and I are doing the same. I have a friend back home whose brother is a deputy here in Moon Ridge. He let me know that Chloe and Rayne haven't left town. No one is getting in or out of town without a car search. I'll let you know what we find."

I left the police station and headed to Moon Ridge Valley High. Our caps and gowns were ready for pick up, so I went to get mine before I became too preoccupied. When I arrived, Reagan was also picking his up as well. I knew that meant he had passed his finals. I was so proud of him. We grabbed our caps and gowns and left to track down Chloe and Rayne. I told Reagan everything I had learned since we last spoke. He knew I was concerned about Logan being transferred to a new facility, so he said, "Logan will be ok. I know that our friend, Logan, would never have stabbed me. He never would have stalked you. I am positive Chloe did something to him, and once we find her, we will have all the answers we need."

"Incoming call from Cassie," Reagan answered his phone via Bluetooth.

"Hey Cass, I'm here with Riley. What's up?"

"Cody and I were talking. We think it would be safer for all of us to ride together."

Reagan looked at me before answering so I nodded in agreement. Reagan dropped his car off in front of the police station to ensure it would be safe. Cody drove to Rayne's house, but when we got there, police were still searching the basement for more clues about Logan's disappearance and captivity. Cody got out of the truck and approached one of the officers. We had no idea what they were talking about, but shortly after their conversation, Cody called us over to him.

"Deputy Jerry said we can look around as long as we don't touch anything."

Since there were police on the scene, we decided to split up to cover more ground. I went with Cody momentarily because I wanted to speak with Deputy Jerry.

"Deputy Jerry, may I ask you a few questions?"

"Sure miss, what would you like to know?"

Cody cleared his throat and sat down on the floor as if he was preparing for a long conversation. I rolled my eyes at him as I pulled my notebook out of my purse.

"Why was Logan being kept here, and how did they keep him here for so long without being caught?"

"Honestly, I'm not sure. From what I've seen, the Scotts were not the friendly, neighborly type. They kept to themselves and never interacted with anyone else."

"Ok, but wouldn't someone notice them bringing Logan here?"

"Not necessarily, I doubt they did it in broad daylight, and if there was no struggle or commotion, I don't see why the neighbors would get involved."

"I guess that makes sense." I replied halfheartedly.

"Any more questions miss?"

Cody chuckled.

"I ignored him and said, "That's it for now. I'll find you later if I have any other questions. Thank you, Deputy Jerry."

Cody held his hand out for me to help him off of the floor. As he began to get up, I let go of his hand. I was frustrated with him, and I wanted to make sure he knew it. He fell backward and slammed his elbow on the wooden plank behind him. I was expecting him to scream, but Cody got up without difficulty or pain. He bent down and knocked on the plank. The sound of the wood was hollow. He knocked on the adjacent planks which were solid. Cody stood up and stomped on the plank causing it to pop out of the floor. Instantly, something beeped.

"Cody, back away slowly." Deputy Jerry walked over to the plank, bent down, and shined a spotlight into the floor.

"Someone get Sheriff Franklin on the phone. He needs to call the bomb squad immediately."

Because we did not know if the bomb was movement-sensitive, we all did our best not to move.

"Deputy Jerry, besides the bomb, what else is in the hole?" I asked.

"From what I could see, just a few pictures, cassette tapes, a letter, and a metronome. Everything is dusty, so I can't really see much more."

After ten minutes, a member of the bomb squad radioed Deputy Jerry.

"Hello, this is Captain Frye from the bomb squad. Who am I speaking with?"

"Jerry of the Moon Ridge Valley Police Department."

"All right Jerry, I assume you've never diffused a bomb before."

"Yeah, that'd be correct."

"Ok, I will tell you what to do, but I need to know what the bomb looks like."

"Um, it's got red, green, and blue wires as well as an off switch."

"An off switch?"

"Yeah, I'm gonna…" The signal went out.

"Hello! Jerry! Jerry, can you hear me? Don't push the switch! Captain Frye shouted.

"Guys, did he just say push the switch?" Deputy Jerry asked slightly bewildered.

"Don't push the switch, Jerry!" Everyone yelled.

"I don't want to die. If you push that switch, we are all dead." I looked around for Reagan because I wanted my last memories to be with him.

"We're not gonna die, Riley. I promise." Cody took my hand and held on tight.

Suddenly, we heard footsteps coming downstairs into the basement.

"Is anyone down there?" A voice said in the distance.

"Reagan, is that you?"

"Yeah Riley, I've been looking for you everywhere."

"Don't come downstairs!" I yelled hoping he would actually listen.

His footsteps came to an abrupt halt.

"Riley, what's wrong? You sound scared. Are you in danger?"

"Yeah, I am. We all are, so stay as far away from the basement as you can." I heard the steps begin to creak.

"Reagan, there is a bomb down here. Take Cassie and get as far away from the house as you can. I'll look after Riley until we get out of here."

"Thanks, Cody, but I'm not leaving my girl."

Nevertheless, Reagan had no other choice but to leave. I heard a quiet voice coming from the stairs, but it wasn't Cassie or Reagan. The voice grew louder.

"Kids. you need to get out of here now!"

"No, take her. I'm not going anywhere."

"Come on, Reagan. Don't be an idiot. It's pointless to argue with the police." Cassie was highly irritated and for good reason. She left Reagan on the stairs arguing with the officer.

Since Reagan wouldn't go willingly, the officer hand to handcuff him and drag him outside. Reagan's screams were piercing to my ears and my heart.

"Get off of me! My girlfriend is down there! I can't leave her! Let me go!"

As Reagan's screams faded, I wondered if I would ever hear his voice again.

Deputy Jerry had grown weary of waiting. He was continually scratching his head while muttering to himself. Finally, he stopped and said, "The timer has three minutes left. Everyone get out! Slowly walk upstairs; once you reach the top, run as quickly as you can."

With the exception of Cody, no one hesitated. "Deputy Jerry, it's not right for you to do this alone."

"Cody, thank you, but the sheriff needs this evidence, and you need to live your life. Get out of here, kid." Deputy Jerry stuck his hand into the floor and pulled out the bomb. "Grab everything you can and run! You've gotta get out now!"

Cody did as he said. Although he hoped Deputy Jerry would make it, Cody's gut said otherwise.

We all waited across the street watching to see when Deputy Jerry and Cody would run outside. The countdown had seconds left. We could hear footsteps running towards the door. Cody came bursting outside with five seconds left. As he was crossing the street, the timer reached zero. We braced for the explosion, but nothing happened. Captain Frye and a few other members of the bomb squad unit went inside to dispose of the bomb and to help Deputy Jerry get out of the house. Less than a minute later, I saw a car that looked identical to Chloe's at the end of the street.

"It's Chloe! hat car belongs to Chloe!" I yelled at the top of my lungs. As I looked at the car, I saw her wave, lift something, and push a button. Instantly, the house exploded into rubble. Chloe took off as the squad cars made it to the end of the street. Squad cars came pouring in from every direction until Chloe was forced to stop. As she stepped out of the car, the officers realized it wasn't a she. It wasn't Chloe. Rayne was wearing her purple wig, and he seemed very disoriented. He kept babbling about needing to push the button. He was taken into custody but was put under 24 hr. surveillance because he was acting like

Logan. Sheriff Franklin hoped that he would finally make a breakthrough in the case.

Cody was devastated by the loss of his friend. Deputy Jerry had been a big part of Cody's life for a very long time. We knew Cody needed time to grieve; he did not need to spend any more time chasing down Chloe. None of us did. Cassie drove Cody home while Reagan and I rode back to the police station with one of the deputies. Before Cody left, we took the evidence from him to see if anything worthwhile was in the pile of junk. On the way to the police station, we looked through everything. There were two cassettes with extremely faded labels, pictures of Chloe and Jadon, a letter from Jadon to Chloe, and a metronome. Upon reading the letter, we realized that Jadon must have broken up with Chloe via the mail. Nonetheless, the things we had in front of us weren't adding up to anything substantial. Right before we pulled up to the police station, I took a picture of everything we were about to hand to the sheriff. Reagan decided to stay in the car while I took the evidence inside.

"Hi Sheriff, Cody was the one who obtained these, but he had to go home. He lost a close friend today."

"I know he did. Deputy Jerry was a good man. He will be missed."

I handed him the evidence and said, "Sheriff, I'm glad we were able to recover these, but my days of chasing criminals are over. I want to help Logan, but this is all too much. I'm gonna spend my last days in Moon Ridge Valley doing the one thing I haven't done in two years."

"And what's that?"

"Being a teenager, sir." I breathed a sigh of relief as I walked out of the police station.

As I got into the car, Reagan said, "So what's next, Riley?"

"Let's go home, watch movies, eat pizza, and hang out like regular teenagers."

Reagan's face lit up with joy. He was thrilled at the thought of taking the night off. When we got home, Cody's truck was parked in front of my house.

"Hey Cody, what's going on?" I asked.

"We didn't want to be alone. Is it ok if we hang out with you guys for a little while?"

"Yeah man, of course. I'll see if Zander and Paisley want to come over. After all, we've got two days left until graduation, so let's make the most of it." Reagan seemed and sounded so carefree, but after the day we had, anyone would be excited to relax. Once Zander and Paisley arrived, we ordered pizza and wings, binge-watched *Mountain Peak Plains*, and danced the night away. It was the best night I had had in a very long time.

Chapter Twelve

It was the day before graduation, and I was looking forward to getting out of Moon Ridge Valley and escaping all of the trouble that plagued me in my small town. I had been accepted into four different universities, but I chose NYU because that was my dream school. Logan and I were planning on going there from the time we were 7 years old, but I would have to go without him. Nonetheless, I would be in the same state as most of my friends and Reagan, and that made me happy.

Reagan was excited for us to go to New York. Because I was bringing so many things with me, my parents and I arranged for them to drive their car, and Reagan was going to drive my car. We were really looking forward to the trip, but we had to make it through graduation and summer first.

On the morning of our graduation, I was so nervous. I hated speaking in front of people, but the salutatorian is required to give a speech. Thankfully, my speech did not have to be as long as Zander's was.

"Knock, knock."

"Can we come in?"

"Of course."

As soon as my parents came into my room, they both became teary-eyed.

"Mom, Dad, please don't cry. You'll make me cry, and my mascara will start to run."

"I can still remember when you first started school. You were only four. I took you to school and brought you to class. You didn't want me to leave, but I had to let you go. Now, it's time for you to leave, and I don't want to let you go."

I was on the verge of tears listening to my dad speak. "Daddy, please don't make me cry."

"I'm sorry baby girl, but I just can't believe you're graduating today. I guess my little girl is not so little."

I hugged my dad and pushed him out of my room.

My mom was silently crying in the corner of my room. I gave her a big hug, but I didn't say a word. I knew I would cry if I did. My mom left my room, and I finished getting ready.

Since I needed to be an hour early for staging and sound check, I left while my parents waited at the house for our family members to show up to our house.

Although I was panicking, being able to read my speech with no one around to judge me made me feel better. As I reached the closing of my speech, I heard clapping coming from behind me. I turned around and saw Reagan. He knew I was scared and uncomfortable, so he came to give me some much-needed encouragement.

An announcement came over the P.A., "Clear the stage. I repeat, clear the stage."

Reagan and I went to the room where our classmates were waiting. It wasn't long before we had to take our seats in the courtyard. The ceremony was about to start, and the seats were filling quickly. My classmates and I took our seats in the courtyard and on the stage. Moments later, the ceremony began. It was really beautiful, but I couldn't wait for it to be over. I just wanted to give my speech and walk across the stage.

"And now presenting, Zander West, our class of 2019 valedictorian."

Zander walked up to the microphone with such confidence and delivered a short, but amazing speech.

"Well guys, we did it. We made it this far, and we'll make it even farther as long as we remember who we are and where we came from. If high school has taught us one thing, it's that we can do anything together. Congratulations class of 2019."

I didn't think Zander would finish his speech so quickly, and before I could gather my thoughts, the applause ended.

"And now presenting, Riley Abernathy, our class of 2019 salutatorian."

I was so nervous. I was sweating and shaking profusely.

"High school has been quite the journey. For some of us, it's been slow and steady, and for others, it's been filled with the most extreme highs and lows. We have overcome so many obstacles and have been through more than most people our age. Although not all of us are here today and not everyone will walk this stage, to the ones of us who are moments away from graduating, congratulations! After everything we have faced, we can make it through anything. We can do anything!"

There was a long pause after my speech. I wasn't sure if they were expecting me to say more or if they thought my speech was awful, but my thoughts were interrupted with the sound of applause. As soon as the applause ended, it was time for us to walk.

"Riley Abernathy...Reagan Alexander...Gabriel Cole...Jadon Cole...Cody Hale...Cassandra Kane...Paisley

Moore…Omar Rodriguez…Brielle West…Zander West."

It was official! We were high school graduates. We finally closed our chapter in Moon Ridge Valley, and we were ready to see what the world had to offer us.

The summer flew by quickly. After months of searching, Sheriff Franklin finally found Chloe. She had been hiding out in a ratty motel on the edge of town. One of the guests saw her filling an ice bucket outside of the motel. He immediately realized she was the girl from the reward posters in the entrance lobby. He called the number on the poster and let Sheriff Franklin know exactly where she was.

Within a few minutes, the building was surrounded by officers. Sheriff Franklin made sure everyone's sirens remained off for the duration of the trip to the motel. When he arrived, he kicked down the front door. Chloe tried to escape out of the back door, but officers were waiting for her when she opened it.

Chloe was finally in police custody, and there was no amount of bail that could get her out. The town was relieved that she had been caught, but no one was more relieved than the Andrews and I were.

Although Logan was not going free, Chloe's capture meant there was a chance for him to be released. Sheriff Franklin knew it would take a while to put the pieces together, but he was more than willing to dedicate all of his time and resources to figuring out what Chloe had done to Logan and Rayne.

The day before moving to New York, I said goodbye to a lot of people, but I saved the most important person for the day of the move.

Reagan came over bright and early. He helped me double-check to make sure I had everything I needed. My parents and his family decided to meet Reagan and me at the Brain Trauma Center where I was going to say goodbye to Logan. Because we had to get on the road, I only had half an hour to spend with him.

It was hard seeing him in the facility especially since he hadn't made much progress. I gave him the biggest hug when I saw him, and although he still didn't look like my Logan, he did look much better.

"Riley, I don't want you to leave, but I know you have to go make your dreams come true. I asked my parents to bring this for you as a going-away present."

He handed me his favorite leather jacket with the hood. "Put it on, Riley. I want to see how it looks on you."

I did as he asked, and for a moment, I saw the light in his eyes that had been missing ever since his return.

He gave me one more hug and said, "I love you, Riles. I always will."

"I love you too, Logan."

I walked down the long hallway ready to leave this town and everyone in it. I shed a few tears over Logan, and I would shed a lot more. Nevertheless, I had hope that he would be better soon.

That would be our last conversation for quite some time. I would later blame myself for not reaching out to him sooner. I didn't know that he had slipped a note in the jacket pocket

right before I left, and I wouldn't find it for a
few years.

About The Author

Ashley Davis was born and raised in Florida but is Barbadian by blood. She is a fun-loving creative soul that enjoys expressing herself through any artistic avenue and has always had a heart for children.

From coaching Little League and teaching, to being a Youth Director, Ashley is no stranger to working with children. She has been making up stories from the time she was a child and has been sharing them with children ever since.

When her Godson, Emery, asked her to turn his bedtime stories into real books, she was uncertain, but after her mother, Verna, (also a published children's book author) overheard Ashley telling stories to Emery, she encouraged Ashley to publish the stories. So, she did.

CHAPTER 31

S tefan stared at the closed door.

"What he says makes no difference." Cerny regarded him with a sly smile. "You can't hope to defeat Nerian."

Thoughts spinning, Stefan barely noted Cerny's remark. Then, Kahar's words hit him. *'They are in the throne room.'* He spun on his heels to face the room's entrance. "No." He whispered. "No." Gut clenching, he sprinted down the hall. When he reached the door, he didn't bother to push, choosing instead to slam it open with his shoulder.

Flames crackled in the braziers next to the pillars and in the three large hearths along the walls. Unlike the rest of the castle, the throne room was hot. Up on the dais, dressed in ebony armor, Nerian slouched, his throne barely visible behind his massive form. On either side of him sat Anton and Celina. There was no sign of Thania.

Cerny rushed into the room. "Sire—"

King Nerian stopped him with an upraised hand. "So the wayward son returns," Nerian's voice echoed throughout the empty chamber. "Children, go greet your father."

They glanced over to Nerian as if uncertain.

"He *is* your father, isn't he? Go on."

They stood. Stefan's eyes widened, and if not for the

circumstances, he would have smiled at how much they'd grown. Anton was almost Stefan's height, his shoulders broad, hair coal–black. Celina was also tall, but she had her mother's silky tresses and dainty shape. Both were dressed in finery. Despite the years, their features were unmistakable.

One foot in front the other, Stefan reminded himself as he willed his feet to move and began to walk toward his children. At first, Anton and Celina took slow, uncertain steps, then their pace quickened, and eventually they ran. Tears in his eyes, Stefan broke into a run to meet them.

"Father," Anton said, breathless when they met near the room's middle. "Is that really you?"

"Yes," Stefan replied. He grabbed them both in his arms and hugged them.

"Of course it is silly," Celina said. "He's almost the same as when Mother lets us see him in her *divya*. The one that resembles him."

The pendant of Thania hanging around Stefan's neck was heavy and cold against his skin. "Yes. Yes it is," he whispered. He hugged them even tighter.

The moment seemed to go on forever, him hugging his children, and they squeezing him in return. They cried the entire time.

Finally, Stefan released them. Wiping at his eyes, he asked, "Where's your mother?"

"She abandoned them," Nerian said from across the room.

How did the King hear what was said from so far away? "She would never do that," Stefan shouted. He searched his children's faces to confirm he was right. Sadness reflected at him.

"She's been gone for days," Anton said.

Celina shook her head, mouth downturned. "The same day Uncle Nerian's King's Guard showed up at our home."

"Uncle Nerian?" Stefan repeated.

Anton shrugged. "It's what we called him for years. Mother said Uncle used to look after you like you were his son."

Stefan took in the throne and the stranger sitting upon it. "That was a long time ago. He's no longer the same man. Did your mother give any idea where she was going?"

"I know, but I doubt they would." Nerian chuckled.

A squeeze of his arm made Stefan look down. It was Anton's hand. When he met his son's eyes, Anton's expression pinched with concentration.

"He cannot hear us now, Father," Celina whispered, lips barely moving. "Anton is making sure of that."

She had positioned herself to block the King's view. The strain on Anton's face revealed the boy was Forging. Stefan nodded to show he understood.

"Mother left when the King sent his Alzari for all of us," Celina said, her voice still low. "By the time she realized what was happening it was too late. We would have fought them off, but there was no way to win. No one knows where Mother went or how she escaped. So we have sat here, playing the innocent niece and nephew to the King while hoping she returns with help. Father ..." Her voice cracked a little. "We're both scared. We saw what the King does to those who fail him. A–And the creatures that stalk these halls, often trying to get in here ... We can hear them growling late at night. We can smell them. A–Anton says they're shadelings."

"They are," Stefan said. "The King has turned to the shade."

Celina sucked in a breath, her gaze darting toward Nerian. A dip of Anton's head and the unsurprised expression on his face said he suspected as much.

"What are we going to do?" Celina asked, her hand gripping Stefan's even tighter, fingers cold and clammy against his palm.

"Enough of the whispering," Nerian called. "Enter."

The double doors to the chamber's left side swung open. In pairs along the shadowy hallway, nine figures entered the room. Stefan's sword vibrated violently against his leg.

The first four were wraithwolves, fur rippling, mouths

lolling in toothy grins.

Darkwraiths entered after them. Long black cloaks hid their bodies, and their feet never appeared to touch the ground. Smoky mist danced around them. It coiled up like a living thing to hide their faces in a translucent hood from which red eyes glowed.

Even as seeing the shadelings here, so obviously under Nerian's command, came as a shock, nothing prepared Stefan for the person trudging between them. His heart felt as if it had been ripped from his chest. Dressed in blue, tattered, bloody clothes, her face a mask of welts was Thania.

"No, no … no … no," Stefan whispered. Fresh tears welled up in his eyes.

The group positioned themselves next to Cerny. A slow, triumphant smile spread across his features. "I told you I would take your place."

Choked cries escaped from Celina and Anton. Stefan managed to prevent them from running to their mother. He did not know how he kept his ground or stood despite the weakness in his knees, but something deep within told him he must.

His pendant bloomed with warmth. He reached a tentative hand to the charm before he stopped. Why hadn't he felt the same from the children? Thania's words rose fresh in his mind. *'Our pendants, the pieces of us I imbued into them, now also contain a part of the children's essences. The day you do not feel its warmth, our love when within its presence is the day you will know something is amiss. But even then, there will be hope.'* He should have realized what the pendant's coldness meant when the children came near, but he was so overwhelmed by his emotions he'd missed its importance.

Stefan made to ease his grip from Celina's, but a warning look flashed across his wife's face.

A chuckle began behind him. The sound built into a hearty laugh. By the time he turned to face throne, it was a cackle.

King Nerian's mad laugh rose to a feverish pitch before he sputtered into silence. The only other noise within the room came from the flames crackling atop the braziers.

"I apologize, but I could not help myself," Nerian said. "The expression on your face when you saw your wife, the way she tried to warn you … This whole scenario is priceless. The deception almost worked too."

"What—" Stefan began.

"Oh, come now," Nerian said. He pointed at Thania. "That … is your wife. Those," he gestured at Anton and Celina, "are not your children."

Stefan's mouth dropped open. Not from surprise that they weren't his children, but because the King had known all along.

Nerian chuckled. "Why the charade? I wanted to witness how this would unfold." His gaze shifted to the children. "If you could tell they were not yours or if they would fool you completely. A good try, Thania. However, when you are as strong as I am in Mater, one can sense the tiny disturbance in the essences that accompanies even the most experienced Sven."

With those words, Nerian gave a lazy wave of his hand in Stefan's direction. Spear–like flames darted from two of the braziers near the King and shot down the room.

Around Stefan, the ground rumbled and heaved. He lost his balance, stumbling for a moment as he noticed the children step forward. Eyes wide with shock and fear, he could do nothing to help.

The spears of fire tore through the air. The children stepped to the side and off the carpet. Serene smiles crossed their faces, then abruptly their arms elongated and flowed down to touch the marble floor. Stone and earth flowed up over them. The flames struck with a low boom.

Stefan threw a hand up against the sudden heat and the small concussion.

Fire rippled around and down the stoneform figures that were once his children. The flames snuffed out as if sucked away by a deep indrawn breath.

In place of Anton and Celina stood two ten–foot Sven. Marble and rock covered their bodies. Smoke rose from them.

The smell of char trickled through the room. Below them, the ground was torn. As one, they roared at the King.

"Calm down." Nerian cocked his head, an amused expression on his face.

The Sven quieted, but their brown-eyed glares remained on him.

"So," Nerian stood, "all the pieces are together. We have the Sven, so I should count the Harnan as well, the Tribunal and their Ashishin, the Felani hiding behind the Vallum of Light waiting for said Tribunal." He chuckled. "Let's not forget the Erastonians."

"All the more reason for you to give up this madness," Stefan said, finally finding his voice. He tried his best to ignore the sword vibrating against his leg. It was a constant reminder the shadelings held his wife.

"Ah, but I hold the advantage." Nerian's gauntleted hand gestured toward his right and a small, dark entryway there.

The door opened. Anton and Celina, eyes fearful, clothing disheveled, shuffled into the room. Kahar glided in after them, his dark cloak and clothing motionless.

"NOOO!" Thania screamed.

Stunned, Stefan opened and closed his mouth.

"Mother," the children cried, trying to head to her. Kahar cut them off.

"Not once did you think the Ashishin assisting your escape would belong to me." Nerian shrugged as if it was obvious to him. "Bring them to me."

Every fiber within Stefan's body urged him to do something. Anything. But what could he do against Nerian, Kahar and the shadelings? Even his wife who was as strong or stronger than any High Ashishin he knew, appeared powerless. Thania had crumpled to the floor, crying.

The children approached the King, their gazes drifting to Stefan. They gasped. Celina began to wail. Anton mouthed the question, "Father?"

Heart thumping as he fought down sorrow, Stefan

nodded. There had to be some way to help his children. "W–What do you want, Nerian? Please, stop this."

"I am almost tempted to say that time has passed," Nerian said. "Come, children, do not be afraid." He beckoned them on as they paused a few feet from the dais.

When they climbed the steps and stood next to him, Nerian glanced from one to the other, his lips curled into a wicked smile. He ruffled Anton's hair, then strode down the stairs, leaving the throne and the children arrayed at his back.

"You were like a son to me, Stefan. All I asked was for your help in fighting the Erastonians, to establish the rule of the Setian. In return, you would rule beside me. What do you do instead? You ally with them."

Stefan fought down the urge not to gape at Nerian's revelation. *How did he find out?*

"You hide your surprise well, Stefan," Nerian said. "But there is little I do not know. Man's greatest flaw is greed. The power of promises and delivering on them."

"Dishonorable use is not what *the Disciplines* were created for."

"Oh? So, you wrote them?" A smirk played across the King's face. "Like anything else, they are a tool. In this case, one that teaches you how to get the best out of your men in whatever endeavor. For example, the Erastonians invaded Seti, already destroyed several towns and cities, massacred hundreds of thousands, and enslaved even more. They managed to defeat the greatest General Seti has ever known. Our armies and our Alzari will fight like never before. Right now, they are slaughtering your precious Erastonians."

This time, Stefan did gape.

"Thank you for bringing them together in one location for me to crush. You served your purpose better than if you hadn't betrayed me." Nerian slowly shook his head from side to side. "And to think, I gave you everything."

"No." A sudden rage boiled in Stefan as he thought about all the dead, all the lives and families shattered over countless years of war. All wasted because he was blind to Nerian's plans all those years. "I earned what I had. Many times over. What you asked was for me to go against what I believed in. All you have taught me. *The Disciplines*, honor, respect for life, and a man's need for family. What happened to you, Nerian?" Stefan gestured to the shadelings. "To make it worse you turned to them, the very thing that has tried to destroy the world for years."

"Nothing happened. I am who I am."

"Lies!" Stefan shouted. "You were an honorable man. A man many admired—even worshipped—as if you were one of the gods. Now, look at yourself, look at your people, look at the filth and darkness that has become of Benez. You're nothing more than a madman deluded by dreams and prophecies of the dead."

Nerian scowled. Then, he shrugged. "Mad, maybe. Deluded? No. There are things beyond your understanding at work here. The world *will* be covered in the shade's darkness. Nothing will stop that. No one is prepared. I will be victorious. But, in order to do so, there is something I need. Your sword. Release its bond to me or I will kill your children."

Stefan stared, not believing the heinous words Nerian uttered. He closed his eyes, a hand sliding to his head to massage where his skull ached. To kill during a war was one thing, but to threaten to murder the children was beyond Stefan's comprehension. Nerian was worse than a lunatic. He was a rabid animal that needed to be destroyed.

However, such a thing was easier thought than accomplished. The King faced the two Sven, Thania, whatever power Anton and Celina could muster, and yet appeared unconcerned. If Nerian wanted, he could probably kill everyone within the room. Not that Stefan was discounting himself, but for him to have any hope, he needed to get closer to the King.

"I served you faithfully all these years," Stefan said, his voice a hair above a whisper. "Giving all I had, helping to build a kingdom, protecting the people and your rule. Not once before did I question your need for glory and conquest. I embraced it, took in what you taught me, and made your wishes a part of myself. All I ever asked was a chance to enjoy the fruit of the blood we spilled if the gods should ever bless me to live that long." He stared longingly at his children. "Now I have that chance, and you not only deprived me of raising my children, but you would take them away from me? Kill them?" The seething inside him bubbled to the surface in a red–hot cauldron. "For a sword?"

"No. Not only a sword," Nerian said from where he stood at the bottom of the dais. "The power within it."

"So for a chance at power you would ask me to choose between the weapon and my blood?"

"I was not asking." Nerian flicked a hand.

Celina made a choking sound. Kicking and thrashing, she rose slowly until she floated several feet above the throne. Her eyes bulged.

"Cel!" Anton yelled, hand outstretched toward his sister. Then he spun on Nerian, his face a mottled mask. Before Anton made another move, he went flying into the throne.

Something tugged at Stefan's feet. Marble slid up to his ankle then hardened. Any attempt he made to shift was futile.

"Nerian," Thania yelled.

Stefan snapped his attention back to his wife

Brow bunched together, she stared down the King, hands clenched into fists. Expression strained, Cerny stepped toward her, fist upraised.

One of the wraithwolves next to Thania exploded. Great gouts of blood and flesh splashed not only its counterparts but on her as well, painting the floor and nearby wall crimson.

Cerny's arm shook. Whatever Forging they were using, they battled mightily against each other.

A second later, Thania's shoulders sagged and her expression changed to one of shock. She sunk to the floor.

With two mighty roars, the Sven pounded their fists into the floor. Marble and stone boiled up around them. The piled debris shot forward and sent flagstones in a rippling wave toward the King. At the same time, the two Sven leaped.

The wave of earth came to a jarring halt as if slamming into an invisible wall. Before they reached the apex of their jumps, the Sven froze. The air within the throne room grew so cold Stefan's teeth chattered. Frost, then ice, rippled across the Svens' giant forms. A moment later, they shattered. A shower of flesh, dirt, and stone fell with their deaths.

Transfixed, Stefan stared in disbelief. To do all he'd accomplished, Nerian would have had to Forge air to lift and bind Celina and create the wall, use light to kill the wraithwolf and Warp the Mater around Thania, reconstitute earth around Stefan's leg, and use water and ice to destroy the Sven. To be a High Matii, one had to be able to wield two of the three elements. But to Forge essences from all three? Simultaneously? Impossible.

The rattle of Celina as she wheezed and coughed, and Thania's low keening moan broke him from his thoughts. The smell of fresh blood and the rot of wraithwolf filled the room. As his mind registered the devastation Nerian wrought, Stefan tried to work out a solution. Even if he got close enough, the King would kill him before he could blink.

One possible course remained to ensure his family survived. He decided to take it.

"I–I will release the sword's bond to you," Stefan said. "J–Just don't hurt them anymore."

"I knew you would come around." Nerian smiled, but he didn't venture closer.

In the King's icy, emerald eyes Stefan saw the truth. When he handed over the sword's bond, Nerian intended to kill them all.

Stefan took in the tear–streaked faces of his children. Then he looked at his wife, her tattered clothing and bruised body. He opened his Matersense. All around her, Cerny, and the shadelings, the elements were Warped. Tentacles of shade spread from Cerny to the shadelings and to the King.

My wife, my children, the only ones I might ever have, taken from me, denied lives of their own. With the thought came heaviness in his heart. As sudden as the grief rose, a mounting anger joined it. The heat of his emotions roiled through him. Another, different burning sensation followed.

"Give me the *divya*."

Nerian's words sounded far away. All Stefan felt was the inferno now throbbing within him. Scouring his insides, it emanated from his anger and one other point. He closed his eyes and threw his head back as the sensation engulfed him.

The second source of fire, of energy, was the sword. The weapon seemed to beckon to his emotions.

When Stefan opened his eyes, Nerian had taken several steps down the colonnade. The King's lips moved but Stefan heard nothing. He strained to make out the words against the roar of the power in his ears.

"With the power your sword holds, the world will be mine." Nerian's eyes had the mad gleam again as he stared lustily at the *divya*.

In desperation, Stefan gave in to the pull. He added the heat of his rage to the energy emanating from the weapon.

"Do not be afraid," Nerian coaxed. "All will be well."

Calm rolled through Stefan as the two blazes joined. "Yes, it will," he answered. He locked gazes with the King. The Svenzar's words of forcing Nerian to create an opening came back to him.

Eyes narrowing, Nerian paused.

A tiny concussion from the sword shot up Stefan's arm. The same as it did the first night in Benez. He recognized how to direct the burst of power now. With a flick of his hand, he sent the energy running through him into the sword and into Nerian's Forging. Marble melted from around his feet. He raised his leg to step toward the King. In the same instant, he spun and leapt the fifty feet separating him and Cerny.

Time took on a miniscule flow. Cerny's eyes widened.

Stefan landed next to the General. He plunged his sword hilt deep into the smaller man's gut and ripped up. Blood spurted, a few drops spattering Stefan's face. Entrails spilled out along with the stench of fecal matter.

"You wanted to replace me," the Knight Commander said with a sense of satisfaction. "Well here, take my sword and unhand my wife." He caught Thania by one arm.

The world sped back up. Cerny crumpled to the floor, blood seeping from his torn torso. The sword protruded from his back, bits of flesh and pulp hanging from its edge.

"What have you—"

The wails from the shadelings cut off Nerian's words. Stefan made to tear his weapon from Cerny's corpse, but the wraithwolves and the darkwraiths dashed toward the King.

A loud crash echoed through the room. Stefan spun to the source of the sound at the throne room's main entrance.

Gouts of fire and light shot down the colonnade. The wind rose in a howl. Through the door stormed at least a dozen High Ashishin. At their head, the air a blur around her fists was Galiana.

"You DARE!" Nerian bellowed. The shield protecting him melted away. He raised his hands.

Stefan prayed he had done enough.

The ground rumbled and the room itself shook. Paintings fell from the walls. Dust, bricks, and mortar dropped from the ceiling.

Between the King and everyone else, the carpeted floor split. Like splintered ice, the crack traveled, as it opened wider until the ground was rent in two. A huge stone hand, covered in tattoos, reached up and grabbed the lip of the chasm. A head followed. Kalvor's head.

The Svenzar pulled himself out of the hole. Six Sven followed, leaping to the lip of the chasm. The earth closed.

Spanning twenty feet, body covered in his tapestry of writhing tattoos, Kalvor almost reached the ceiling. The creature pointed a massive sword at the King, its shiny surface highlighted by glyphs and runes. "The time has come for your madness to end, Nerian. Our kind was not made to bring suffering but to save the world."

A confused expression spread across Nerian's face. He threw both hands up toward the creature. Other than the King's cloak billowing behind him, nothing happened. His face darkened. "You know nothing, Svenzar," he yelled. "You shall fall. All of you will. Kahar, kill the children."

"NO!" Stefan screamed. "I rel—" His words cut off. Something filled his mouth.

Beside him, Galiana appeared.

Nerian roared and the world became a blinding white.

Heat scalded Stefan's skin. A hand pushed him in the chest. Everything went from white to a stark black. A sensation, as if he fell backwards from a cliff into unfathomable depths, swallowed him.

As he spiraled, his gaze was riveted on Kahar. The bodyguard was standing over Anton with his sword in hand. Blood dripped from its edge.

CHAPTER 32

Stefan lurched to a stop. Warm air, too warm for Seti, bright light, and the smell of grass, greeted him. Frowning, he peered around.

A wall rose behind him, spanning several hundred feet into the air. Steel, feldspar, and white alabaster shone with an ethereal glow that lit up the surrounding landscape as if it were daytime instead of night. The Vallum of Light.

Then, like a bucket of freezing water splashed over a man while he slept, the shock of what happened hit him. "No, no … what did you do?" Tears streamed down his face.

"I did what I had to," Galiana's voice said from a few steps to his right.

"T–the children … I … I was going to save them." Unable to hold back, he broke into sobs. "Thania, Celina, Anton … dear Ilumni, why? Why? WHY?" Before he realized, he was on his knees, pounding the ground with his fists.

"I tried," Galiana said, "but we couldn't breach his barrier once he erected it again. We only managed to save you and Thania."

"What?"

"Your wife is over there."

Stefan's gaze followed to where she pointed. An Ashishin fussed over his wife, trying to get her into a gold robe. Her bruised face was already mended. He stood on shaky feet and stumbled toward her.

"Thania, love," he said as she glanced up when he approached.

She scrubbed at her cheeks, her eyes puffy and red. She broke into a wail. "Stefan ... the children ... they're ..." Thania clutched at the pendant around her neck.

"No, you're wrong," Stefan said.

Even as he said the words, he remembered Kahar and his sword dripping with blood. The pendant told the story too. The metal felt incomplete, almost as if a part of him, a part of his soul was missing.

His children were dead.

He took his wife into his arms. Together, they cried.

Several days later, Stefan stood upon the battlements of one of the two Bastions of Light. The tower and its twin looked out over the lone passage through the Vallum here in Felan. His heart ached in ways he never dreamt possible, but his need for revenge was a salve for his pain. Below him, a massive army gathered. The Lightstorm banners flew in too many places to count. A cool wind ruffled his cloak and brought him the scent of perfume.

"If he knew you lived, he would come after you," Galiana said from behind him.

Stefan didn't bother to turn. He couldn't bear to look at her face. "You knew all along he intended to kill them. Why didn't you get them away from Seti?"

"He would not stop hunting all of you if we did," Galiana said. "He was not going to harm Thania, but there was no way to stop him. If he forced you to release the sword to him, he could use the same *divya* we command during our age Forging. Only the gods know what he would be capable of then."

"Do you really think he'll believe I'm dead?"

"The bodies the Sven left cannot be affected in any way. Not even to sense if they are fakes. The power Nerian released made it impossible to identify them beyond a doubt. The man so believes in his own strength I am willing to bet he will convince himself you died."

"And the sword?"

"He will believe we have it."

"How could one man be so strong?" Stefan asked.

"We are unsure if he is simply a man."

"What is he then? A god?"

"Not likely," Galiana said.

"How are you so sure? He used the Streams, Flows, and the Forms. All three elements, Galiana, at one time." Stefan stared down at the army as portals opened to allow in more soldiers, these bearing flags from other Ostanian nations. "He Forged essences from all three elements at once," he repeated to himself yet again.

"There have been quite a few occurrences of late, of old powers seen only in the greatest days of Materforging," Galiana said. "The Chronicles predicted this as a herald to a time of darkness. As for being a god, the Svenzar managed to wound Nerian. I do not believe anyone but the Eztezian Guardians or another of their own could hurt one of the gods."

"Maybe Kalvor was an Eztezian and Nerian a god." Stefan suggested.

"I doubt that. The seals on the Nether are intact. Besides, the day the gods return is the day the world crumbles or so the Chronicles say. The Tribunal suspects it's more likely that Nerian is a Skadwaz."

Stefan shook his head in disbelief. That was just as bad. The Skadwaz had been created with the sole purpose of fighting the Eztezians. "So he isn't dead then?"

Galiana shook her head. "No. The Svenzar and the High Shin failed."

"So my children's lives were wasted."

"Believe me," Galiana implored. "We had no other choice."

"And to think you had my wife go along with this." Stefan shook his head.

"I have told you and Thania has told you … it was her idea."

"To sacrifice our children for a sword?"

"Nerian may have twisted words," Galiana said, "but he did not do so about your sword. The key to our future lies with the *divya*. Would you rather your children be alive and the world destroyed?"

"Yes," Stefan said. "I would give the world for them."

"They would still be dead. So I know you do not mean that."

"Oh, I do. I would give my life and anyone else's for theirs."

"That is grief and your love for them talking," Galiana said. "Regardless, what has happened cannot be changed. You must go on living now."

Stefan frowned. "Why must I?"

"Nerian will still search for the sword. He will hunt any of the Dorn bloodline for a chance to find someone who can activate its power. The Tribunal plans to lead him on a merry chase fed by rumor, but he will find no more Dorns. You are the last."

"So?"

"According to the Chronicles, only one of the Dorn line can bring about the sword's true power. You can use the weapon to some extent, but by now, you should realize you are not the one. Which means you will have at least one more child."

Stefan's heart leaped at the propsect, but images of Celina and Anton tempered his brief elation. "In case you didn't notice, I'm close to the end of my life span."

"We can extend that," Galiana said. "Do you remember when I told you of the bargain to secure a future for what was left of the Setian?"

"Yes. You kept something back that day, as you always do."

"Thania is the key to our age Forging. Of all the Matii we know, only she can combine the essences needed. I should not be the one to tell you this, but in ways she feels she has betrayed you over the years."

Stefan frowned. "Betrayed me? How?"

"Kinai is the key to the Forge. By having people drink a brew made by her, your wife can then use the *divya* I spoke of to tap into their essences as one pool. She can then give access to that power and with it, the maintenance of youth."

Now, Stefan understood. Thania had used this Forging on him to add to his youth. She also encouraged him to make his men drink kinai. Not only did they gain strength from the brew, but his wife extended their lives while providing Nerian and the Council with what they needed. Somehow, he was not surprised. But that was not what bothered him the most. "She was the deciding factor in the bargain to save the Setian," he said. "Without her agreement to give of herself, to use this gift of hers, we would be no more. Not only that, but Nerian needed her also. He was never planning to kill her. Chances are I could have led them from Seti long ago." The full brunt of what his wife had given stuck Stefan like a hammer blow. Tears trickled down his face. "She stayed to ensure we stopped him."

"Yes," Galiana said.

"We failed."

"Not really. Once we made our agreement with the Tribunal, they revealed they had another *divya* similar to the one we used. We shall set up your new home close by in Granadia."

"Fine," Stefan said. The chance to rebuild pulled at him. "After I help defeat Nerian's armies."

"I am afraid that cannot be."

This time, Stefan did turn to face her. He clenched his fists.

"Like I said before, he must never discover that you live." Galiana stared at him, unflinching. "You can help with strategy in the coming war, but you will play no active part. After Nerian has been defeated, you can do as you wish. Until then the fact you and Thania are alive must remain a secret."

Self-mastery, Stefan reminded himself out of habit. He eased his hand away from his sword. He had lost his children, now he was losing a chance for revenge. What other curses did the gods have in store? He turned and continued to watch the army.

The fetid stench of death mixed with sulfuric fumes rose up from the chasm. Howling winds whipped at Kahar's cloak. Heat spilled across his face where he stood at the edge of the precipice. Not far from him, Nerian stared down into the black depths. Several feet behind the King stood High Shin Clarice.

The Great Divide certainly lived up to its name. It was a gaping rent in the earth, several thousand feet wide and gods only knew how deep, stretching north and south until it disappeared. Vines and massive roots grew from the side nearest them. Jagged stone jutted out here and there. The occasional bleached bones were the only color that broke up the monotony of darkness.

Today, Nerian wore a simple shirt and trousers. He had the sleeves rolled up to expose the intricate tattoos twining about his arms. His hand rested on a scabbard at his hip, in which was a massive greatsword. The weapon suited his eight–foot frame. Runes and glyphs covered the hilt.

"It is time," a musical voice said from behind them.

The Svenzar from the Royal Palace stepped up beside them, its twenty–foot stoneform now reduced to about half its size. In the throne room, the creature had not attempted to stop Kahar from killing the children. However, it had blocked Nerian's power from scouring everyone else in the room. An odd thing that. The Svenzar had also provided Nerian with the sword. Stranger still.

All this time, they had followed the Chronicles, believing the key they needed was the one Stefan now held. But this Svenzar, no, this Eztezian Guardian, the beings created by Kahar's own brethren to defeat the gods, had shown them differently. According to the Svenzar, the sword was the one Nerian sought.

Kahar harbored no doubts the creature was right. The Eztezians themselves wrote the Chronicles. In his endeavors here in this realm, he never expected to garner help from one of the ancient Guardians without having to manipulate them as he had Nerian. To his surprise, the Svenzar had offered its help willingly.

The assistance made Kahar wary.

After a deep breath, Nerian unsheathed the sword. He held the *divya* out before him where the sunlight glinted off its surface. Then he leaped off the precipice.

Kahar kept his gaze fixed on the King until the blackness devoured him. Moments, later there was a flash of light and a hollow boom. Essences spilled up from the hole in a thick bar, their power buffeting Kahar. They shot up into the air, turning the blue sky dark.

The essences were of the purest shade.

Below, Kahar noted movement like some disturbed nest of ants or bees.

Shadelings.

Thousands of them. Tens of thousands. Nerian had broken whatever seal had trapped them within the Great Divide.

A flash of shade and light shot up the chasm and landed several hundred feet from Kahar. Energy essences hummed as the mixture resolved into the King. He flicked his hand out and all along the edge of the chasm portals of Materialization opened. Wraithwolves and darkwriaths crawled up from the Great Divide's lip and massed before them. Through the portals' hazy surfaces, a battle between Erastonians and Stefan's forces played out.

Another type of shadeling climbed up behind the others. This one stood on four spindly legs, slender body rippling with sinew. Claw–tipped appendages stuck out from its chest. Two small wings hummed on the creature's back. Thick locks of a fleshy substance hung down past its shoulders. Many–faceted, lidless eyes and dripping mandibles squirmed in a face contorted by masses of black folds. By the hundreds, the daemons spread among their lesser counterparts. They stretched, shade bubbling up around them as they practiced the Forgings to take a human's soul.

The Svenzar grunted and his form began to dissolve into the earth. "And so begins the reign of Nerian the Shadowbearer."

Glossary

Alzari – Matii who wield mostly the Forms, strongest in earth essences and metal. Ancestors of the Setian.

Amuni – One of the gods of Streams, specifically, shade. Brother of Ilumni.

Ashishin – Matii who serve the Tribunal and often represent the god Ilumni and the Streams, specifically light and heat. Most of the Granadian peoples are descendants of the Ashishin. They often bear the title of Shin or High Shin.

Astoca – A kingdom within south central Ostania. Their people, the Astocans, are cousins to the Cardians. (See Namazzi)

Bana – A kingdom in eastern Ostania. Their people are the Banai and worship Humelen and the Forms.

Bastions of Light – Towers along the Vallum of Light and located at strategic points within Granadia that can be used to send warning of an impending attack to the Tribunal.

Cardia – A kingdom far south in Ostania. Their people, the Cardians, are related to the Astocans. (See Namazzi)

construct – A sentient entity created from essences.

Dagodin – A Matus who cannot Forge but can wield items imbued with Mater called divya.

Darkwraith – A type of shadeling created by merging the sela essences, spirit, and shade of a Matus.

dartan – A massive beast of burden, bigger than any horse. It has 6 legs, hardened skin, and a shell into which it can withdraw its legs. It also has a long snake-like neck and is a meat eater. Originally created during the Luminance Wars.

Deathbringer – A type of Matii used by the Felani and others, said to be already crazed Matii. Only the Felani know how they're controlled.

Denestia – The world where this story takes place, said to have been the crowning achievement of the god Ilumni who defeated his brother Amuni for its possession.

Devout – A priest who serves Ilumni and goes on pilgrimages to do the Tribunal's bidding, often preaching the word of Streamean worship and its virtues.

divya – An item imbued with Mater.

Dosteri – A race originating in Everland who later inhabited Granadia.

Elements of Mater – The completed essences that make up the Flows, the Forms, and the Streams. (See Mater)

Erastonia – A kingdom in Everland.

Erastonian – Powerful warriors from Everland, specifically from a place called Erastonia. They possess some of the strongest Matii within the known world. Their main task is defending the Great Divide and killing any shadelings that happen to escape from the prisons contained with the Divide.

Essences – The individual strands of power that make up the elements of Mater.

Everland – The northernmost continent in Denestia.

Exalted – Mythical leaders of the Tribunal.

Eztezian – The Eztezians were the descendants of the gods. Great warriors and the most powerful Matii to grace Denestia. They were tasked with protecting Denestia from the shade and from itself. Driven mad by their overuse of Mater however, they almost destroyed the world. They created the Great Divide, which brought about the shade's defeat. Then they turned on the gods, sealing them in the Nether to prevent future wars and the creation of more creatures like the shadelings.

Felan – A kingdom is western Ostania. Their people are known as the Felani.

Flowic – The religions named after the elements of Flows and its gods.

Flows – The combination of two essences—primarily water and air that make up liquids known as the Flows. There are other variations that involve other essences. E.g Water and cold to form ice. Heat, air, and something flammable to create fire.

Forger – A Matus who can Forge essences of Mater

Forging – See Materforging

Formist – The religion named after the elements of Forms and its gods.

Forms – The combination of three essences—earth, metal, and wood, that make up solids known as the Forms. There are other variations of solids that can be enhanced by using other essences, as well as other essences not in this umbrella that can be used to form solids. (See example in Streams.)

Gerde – Stoneform beasts with eight-legs that bear similarities to crabs, but were the size of ponies.

Granadia – The Western continent of Denestia. Have been at conflict with most of Ostania for millenia.

Harna – A kingdom in northern Ostania. Followers of Formist religion. Descendants of the Sven.

Humelen – One of the Gods of Forms, specifically earth.

Hydae – A world formed by Amuni when he lost to his brother Ilumni.

Ilumni – One of the gods of Streams, specifically, light. Brother of Amuni.

Imbuer – A Matus who can imbue properties of essences into an item to create divya.

kinai – A special plant that draws on essences, used in many healing formulas and potent drinks. Said to enhance the user's strength, stamina, and agility.

Luminance War – An ancient war when shadelings escaped the Great Divide and swept across Ostania.

Mater – Mater is the core elemental power which exists within everything. It makes up the three elements the gods represent and their individual essences. Mater drives all worlds. The three elements are the solids of the Forms, the liquids of the Flows, and the energy of the Streams. Those are further broken down into separate essences. For instance, earth, wood and metal are a part of the Forms. Heat, cold, light and shade are a part of the Streams. Water and air are a part of the Flows. Finally, there's sela essence, a combination of life and death which sits outside the three elements and is required for anything to live or die. (See Streams, Flows, Forms.)

Materialize – Ability to Forge a portal between two places for travel.

Materforging – The act of wielding the essences or elements of Mater.

Matersense – The ability to open up one's mind to be able to sense or see nearby essences within the elements of Mater.

Matus – One who can sense Mater (Plural – Matii) Not every Matus can manipulate or Forge Mater. What essence a Matus is strongest in is often determined by bloodline. However, one can train to become adept in other essences. It is difficult and takes powerful Matii to wield essences from two separate elements simultaneously. It is considered to only be an ability of the netherlings or gods to wield all essences within all three elements at the same time.

Mystera – Schools built throughout Granadia for the purpose of teaching and recruiting Matii.

Namazzi – Matii who wield mostly the Flows, ancestors of the Cardians and Astocans.

Netherling – Primordial beings from the Nether, said to have been the ones to bestow their power on the Eztezians in order to save the world. This act was part of their revenge against the gods for their experiments.

Ostania – The Eastern continent of Denestia. Have been at conflict with most of Ostania for millenia.

Pathfinder – Powerful Matii, trained by the Tribunal,

who have passed the ultimate tests of control over their emotions, which ensure they will not succumb to the temptations of the power the essences promise. They are used to hunt Matii who break the laws governing the use of Forging or those who go insane. They often accompany Ashishin to protect the Ashishin from attackers and from themselves.

Raijin – An elite assassin corps within the Tribunal.

Sanctums of Shelter – Similar to the Bastions of Light but more powerful and arrayed along the mountains in Northern Granadia to protect from any direct incursion by the shade through the Great Divide.

Scorpio – A massive crossbow–type weapon that fires large metal projectiles.

Senjin – A sport played with a leather ball, featuring 14 combatants, 7 per side, on a field spilt into 6 parts, with two halves. The team to score three times first, wins.

Seti – A kingdom in north western Ostania. Their people the Setian are descendants of the Alzari. (See Alzari)

Shadelings – Creatures created in the God Wars, primarily by the god Amuni, and his followers by experimenting with netherlings and the essence of shade. The effects of the couplings can be seen within some of the strange beasts within Denestia.

Shin – The respectful title given to Ashishin Matii.

Shunyata – A place within each person where they can separate and control their emotions. Also the place where sela essence is stored within any living being. Also known as the Eye.

Streamean – The religion named after the elements of Streams and its gods.

Streams – The combination of four essences—light, heat, cold, and shade that make up energy. The energy can be used in the forming of the other elements e.g cold is needed to form ice which is part of the Forms and part of the Flows.

Sven – The earth elemental peoples that inhabit the Nevermore Mountains in north eastern Ostania. Descendants of the Svenzar.

Svenzar – Form elementals that reside in mountainous areas. Their power resides in earth, metal, and wood.

The Aegis – Said to be a power or a person who would help either protect the gods or defend against their resurgence.

The Chronicles – Said to be sacred tomes written by the Eztezians themselves and their descendants, dictating the past and the future of the world.

The Disciplines – A set of rules and pointers on how to govern and lead soldiers.

The Eye – See Shunyata.

The Great Divide – A massive rift in the land created by the Eztezians to defeat the shadelings. It runs from north to south across central Everland, and is guarded by the Erastonians.

The Iluminus – Named after the god Ilumni, it is the central city, learning hub and home of the Tribunal and its Matii.

The Nether – A realm between the worlds thought to be the origination of Mater, the gods, and netherlings.

The Stone – The great hidden city where the Svenzar and Sven live in northern Ostania.

The Unvanquished – Stefan Dorn's elite troops in Ostania.

Travelshaft – Tunnels developed by the Svenzar using the Forms, where time is slowed and speed increased to allow travel between large distances in a small amount of time. Said to somehow be constructed between the Planes of Existence.

Tribunal – The founding society of Ashishin among the Matii. They determined what was needed for the Matii as a whole to function in their proper roles as protectors and mediators. Eventually, the different Matii split apart due to conflicts in ideals, philosophies and religions. The Tribunal rules in Granadia. They left Ostania where most of the other Matii fled, to fend for themselves.

Vallum of Light – A massive wall imbued with Mater and erected by Eztezians within the Tribunal to separate Ostania from Granadia.

Warping – A Forging by powerful Matii, using the sela

essences of something recently killed, to twist the essences in a specific area, thus rendering them unusable for a period of time.

Wraithwolf – A type of shadeling using a combination of wolf or other canine type beast, as well as the sela of a person, and essences of shade.

Zar – The respectful title given to Alzari Matii.

ETCHINGS OF POWER

Aegis Of The Gods Book 1

The opening stanza in a new epic fantasy series that delves into the themes of war, corruptible power, love, betrayal, and absolution in the world of Denestia.

Ryne Waldron, a living legend at the edge of madness is haunted by a murderous past and the voices of his power that whisper in his head. Hunted, he strives to defend a village he swore to protect. But his enemies might be closer than he could ever suspect.

Ancel Dorn, a gifted student, struggles with rejection and must accept who he is or perish to the creatures that stalk him and his parents. When he discovers he's targeted for death by beings that seemed to have stepped from the history of an ancient war, his only choice is to flee.

Irmina Nagel, Ancel's former lover, and an assassin sent to find Ryne, is mired in her quest for revenge on Ancel's parents, and must set aside her emotions or fail her final test. What she discovers may not only change her life but the world as a whole.

Caught between warring nations, vengeful leaders, magic and steel, myth and men, the fate of millions hang in the balance. Who can unite the kingdoms against a common threat? Who shall bring the power that drives the world to heel? Who will walk the knife's edge of harmony? If none can, then Denestia is doomed.

Chapter 1

Ryne Waldron wondered if he should kill the woman. Blood, bodies, and screams rolled across his mind with the thought of her and those she represented. The stink of something dead or worse hung in the air. He expelled a great breath, chest heaving with the hope the stench was only death.

An old, familiar feeling, like heat seeping into a cold hearth, stirred deep within his eight–foot frame. In response, the vibrant tapestry of tattoos covering his body from foot to chin writhed. Seamless replicas of the same artwork decorated his armor, they too twitching in unison with those on his body. Ryne flinched, his muscled arms and broad back clenching, the scars under his leather armor drawing taut. Frowning, he stopped himself from reaching to his hip for his greatsword's hilt. His bloodlust had never risen before unless he touched his power. He shut away the craving to kill with practiced ease.

Unable to shrug off the lapse of control, Ryne stepped to the rear of one of Carnas' many rosewood and teak homes and glanced out across the Orchid Plains. Shimmering heat rose in waves, and yellowed grass and flowers bowed under the sun's rays as if praying for relief, but sure enough, there she stood.

Mariel—if that was even her real name—kept her gaze trained in his direction. Dark hair hung to her shoulders, and she was dressed in a short–sleeved shirt and close–fitting trousers, her slight body and paler skin color the opposite of the native Ostanians. As usual, she stayed beyond the range where he could read her aura.

Ryne turned his head to the noise of a boot scraping on the wooden stairs next to him.

"See here?" Dren craned his head to peer at Ryne, his leather boot poking at a dried bloodstain. "This is where they took Miss Corten last night."

Looming over Dren, although the sinewy man stood two stairs higher, Ryne inspected the scuffmarks. Rust colored splotches stained the wood. Next to the steps, several flattened flowers were the only other signs of a struggle. Ryne's brow wrinkled. "Nowhere near enough blood to have been anything serious."

"Exactly." Dren nodded, scarred hands rising to stroke his short beard. "Miss Corten can hunt as well as any one of us scouts. But no one heard her sound an alarm or even cry out."

Ryne gauged the proximity to the other adjoining homes. Despite the space between houses afforded here at Carnas' outskirts, someone should have heard Miss Corten. With the recent hot weather and lack of rain, the shuttered windows on these houses would've been open. Neither the sturdy structures nor the wooden tile roofs would have kept out the sounds of the struggle or a cry for help. Not even the gales that often howled during one of the frequent thunderstorms could have drowned out Miss Corten's cries. However, there hadn't been any such wind, not the past few days. The weather had remained as it was now, hot, still, and silent with not much more than an inconsequential breeze.

Shifting uncomfortably in his fitted leather armor to sample the air once more, Ryne flicked his thumb across his nose as the whiff of something long dead, of decay and unwashed dog fur curdled his insides. "Have you noticed the smell, Sakari? It's faint, but it's there."

Sakari glided forward, his nostrils flaring. The silver flecks dominating the whites of his eyes flashed as he sniffed the air.

At near seven feet—almost reaching Ryne's shoulder—today he was the opposite of Ryne in girth, his body svelte, each part fit in near perfect proportions under his scaled leather armor. "Yes," Sakari answered after a final scrunch of his nose, "Rot. Old fur. Something not quite dead."

Dren's brows drew together, his eyes narrowed, and sweat beaded his forehead. His hand eased down to his sword hilt as he glanced around, his gaze searching the woods across the expanse of pastures. "Master Waldron, you think it's a beast from the Rot?" the scoutmaster whispered, his head shifting from left to right as if to make sure no one overheard.

Indeed, Dren had cause for his fear. If any beast had crossed the Rotted Forest, there would be reason to worry for everyone. "Maybe. We'll know soon enough. Take us to the body," Ryne ordered.

Dren gave a tentative nod and set off at a jog, his hand on the pommel of his sheathed short sword. Under too clear skies and a burning sun, they cut across the Orchid Plains with its grasses and namesake blue and red flowers that lit up the air with the sweet scent of their blooms. In places, the brush and plants around them not only drooped and were becoming sickly yellow but were a dying brown.

Ryne spared a look over his shoulder, and the muscles along his neck formed a tight rope of tension. As usual, Mariel followed. He smirked. She wouldn't escape him today.

Seeing her usual dogged pattern brought questions rising within Ryne again. Why did she seek him? Why did she maintain the distance from him that she did, yet still followed wherever he went? Could she know of his ability to see auras? No. He dismissed the thought. Besides Sakari, no one else knew.

Brow creased from both curiosity and worry, he wondered if she recognized him. If she did, and she reported his identity to her masters, life would become even more dangerous for Carnas' residents. There wouldn't be just eight villagers who went missing over the last few weeks since she appeared; the Granadian Tribunal would wipe Carnas from the map. The fact he still lived was an embarrassment that reeked of their failure, a weakness for others to exploit.

Or so they would see it.

As soon as the thought crossed his mind, a memory bloomed. Garbed in golden armor of interlocking plates, five–foot greatsword in hand, ebony hair tied in a ponytail, Ryne stood atop a mound of dead people. Skulls and ruptured bodies by the hundreds spread all around a smoke–shrouded village square. He plunged the Tribunal's Lightstorm battle standard through a corpse, into the ground, and roared a challenge. He was the Tribunal's instrument of vengeance and none could stand before him. Not even the Tribunal's own. Then he was running, and running, and running, chased by the Tribunal's assassins. The vision shifted. He was on his knees in chains, unable to use his power, his body covered in blood, torn flesh and half–mended scars from lashes. The whip struck again. Pain seared through his body with the memory. Ryne clenched his sword's hilt. *Never again. Never again will I suffer at the hands of the Tribunal's kind.*

"I see Mariel is still following you. When last you tried to catch her?" Dren's words broke Ryne from his thoughts.

Ryne gave a shake of his head and grunted before he shortened his strides in an effort not to outpace the much shorter man. "Two days ago." Counting his steps, Ryne pictured where Mariel would be behind them. The moment needed to be perfect.

"She's better at hiding than anyone I ever met." The admiration in Dren's voice was clear. "In my years as a scoutmaster, I've yet to meet one as skilled as she who wasn't an Alzari. It's almost like she uses the shade to hide. I wonder if she wields the elemen—"

Ryne veered off from the path the scoutmaster set and broke into a full out sprint, his hand on his scabbard to keep it in place. To his right Sakari kept pace, sandy hair bouncing to match his languid strides, a constant shadow hovering somewhere near, eyes seeing everything but revealing nothing. As Ryne expected, Mariel turned tail and sped toward the Fretian Woods.

With the path clear ahead, Ryne opened his mind and linked with Sakari. Ryne's vision doubled. In one sight, he was in his own body, tearing through the brush. In the other, he saw through Sakari's eyes as if he ran in his companion's boots, each step a glide that barely touched the ground.

"Whatever we do, we must catch her before she reaches the woods," Ryne said under his breath.

"As you wish."

Ryne closed the link, and his vision receded to his alone once more. Ponytail slapping against his back, he ate up the distance between him and Mariel. Frightened birds flapped from his path, their morning song interrupted, protesting squawks coming in discordant jangles.

Dren's unfinished question had brought up another issue Ryne had considered. Suppose Mariel did use the elements to hide? That would make her more than the high ranked priestess she claimed since she arrived in Carnas. Lips curling, Ryne snarled and pumped his massive legs faster. The old pain from his torture by the Tribunal rose anew. If she did possess the ability to use the same power as he, then he would force her to do so. When she did, she would confirm his suspicions of her intent. And he would kill her.

Deep inside himself, Ryne's bloodlust flared to life. In response, his Scripts—the tattoos covering his body— roiled like living things.

Down a gentle slope they ran, the occasional tree a blur as they pursued. On the opposite incline, Mariel crested the hilltop before she disappeared down the other side.

As he rushed to the top of the hill, Ryne's strides faltered and slowed. He'd chosen what he thought was the perfect moment and the best path to cut her off. Somehow, the woman had anticipated his move. Not only had she opened up more distance since the chase began, but she fled at an angle that made sure she would reach the woods long before he managed to catch her. So clear was her path and wide her distance, not only was catching her near impossible, but he wouldn't be able to close the gap to read her aura.

Unless…

He growled in frustration, and his bloodlust surged.

"Embrace your power," a deep voice, steeped in malevolence, whispered in his head. *"Capture her. Kill her."*

"No. Remember what that *has cost you in the past,"* warned a soothing voice in a low whine. *"The blood, the bodies, the innocents slaughtered."*

"Yessss," the first voice encouraged in trembling tones of a creature savoring its pleasure. *"Remember the past. How your power saved you. Our power. Kill for ussss. Feed ussss. And none can escape you."*

The opposing voice pleaded, *"No, please, no. If you do so, you will lose yourself yet again. Is that your wish? To see all you love covered in blood by your hands, steeped in despair that you wrought?"*

On and on the voices warred. Ryne closed his eyes and inhaled deeply, the argument a buzz in the background. As he had practiced the last few years, he listened to the latter voice. If he touched his power now, not only would he kill Mariel, but if he lost control, those he'd come to love in Carnas would suffer a similar fate. Shuddering with the effort, he fought down his lust and shut it off yet again. He heaved a sigh. This sudden rise of his urges didn't bode well. Suspicion of Mariel's ill intentions was all well and good, but without proof, he was no better than those in Carnas who blamed the woman for the missing villagers or the recent bodies they'd found.

What was he thinking? Regardless of her capacity in her work for Granadia's Tribunal, should anything happen to her, Carnas' inhabitants would pay. The Tribunal's price was always absolute. Ryne squeezed his eyes shut for a moment. Picturing those he loved in Carnas lying dead under the Tribunal's banners, crushed by the boots of their military might brought bile rising to his throat.

"Sakari, stop," Ryne shouted. He churned to a halt, his breathing heavy with exertion.

Sakari slowed to a walk. He turned and glided back to Ryne in those smooth strides of his. As he drew close, Sakari shook his head. "You make this more difficult than it needs to be." The green pupils of his eyes were deep pools of nothingness.

Ryne ignored the man. He'd heard the same more than enough times. Well ahead of them, Mariel reached the woods' rosewood and mahogany trees and vanished among the dappled shadows cast by trunks and branches. Ryne spared a glance for the footsteps thudding behind him.

Breaths coming in harsh gasps, Dren caught up with them. "W–What was that all about?" His chest heaved as he gathered himself. "Why chase her now?"

Ryne shrugged." I thought I'd be able to get her before she reached the woods."

Dren wheezed a laugh. "I've seen that bitch easily outrun our dogs. Forian and the others have been whipping the village into a frenzy since you been gone the last two days." He sucked in a breath. "He been saying the things she does proves she's evil. They say she follows the path of the shade."

"And the mayor has been allowing him as usual," Ryne concluded.

Dren nodded. "There's others who think differently, but sooner or later they're going to attack Mariel. May be a good idea for you to speak to them before it gets any worse. They're meeting at Hagan's right now."

"Yes. I might have to," Ryne said, expression thoughtful, his gaze focused on the area where Mariel had fled. She reappeared at the forest's edge. "Lead us to the body," he said to Dren.

Gesturing toward where Mariel now stood, Dren grunted and shook his head. "She sure is persistent." He turned to lead them back the way they'd come.

After one last look at Mariel, Ryne followed Dren with Sakari in tow. Within an hour, the wood–tile roofs and sturdily built homes of Carnas dwindled behind them to the south as they passed the sparse trees dotting this section of the plains. Dren called for them to stop at a small stand of trees. Ryne glanced back. From the edge of the copse, the lone sandstone structure of Hagan's Inn stuck up from the dip in the land where Carnas was located. Near the slope's crest behind them, Mariel watched, but made no attempt to venture closer.

"The body's just in there." Dren pointed to a few stunted kinai trees. The sweet fruit from the misshapen branches dotted the ground, their color yellowed and pale instead of their normal red.

Hand on his sword, Ryne strode toward the kinai orchard with Sakari flanking him. Ryne picked out an old blood trail and smelled the stink of death before he saw the body. Ravaged beyond recognition like the others, the corpse had been stripped naked, limbs twisted at odd angles. From the mess for a face and the torn torso, he could barely tell the person was a man.

Grinding his teeth, his nose upturned at the stench of offal, Ryne inspected the death wounds without touching the remains. The shredded flesh across the corpse's face made Ryne brush the old scars that striped the left side of his own. What did this? Could Mariel be responsible like some suggested? And if so, how? He knew every creature within the woods. None came to mind that could have torn a person in such a way. Something from the Rotted Forest, maybe? No. His Scripts hadn't warned him that his wards had been triggered.

He longed to touch his power to see if any malevolence existed within the gashes or the body, but the potential consequences stopped him. Until he figured out why his control appeared to wane, he needed to resort to relying on his physical gifts. Old habits died hard, and this dead body reminded him too much of his past, of the War of Remnants, of the years before when he'd seen beasts ravaged in even worse ways totter to their feet and attack. A simple method existed for him to make certain no such darkness existed here.

Ryne unsheathed his greatsword with a rasp of metal on leather. Runes and glyphs etched into the five–foot silversteel weapon glinted from the sun's penetration through the trees. In a smooth motion, he stepped forward and swung. The wide, double–edged blade passed through the corpse's neck without resistance. Blood pooled onto the soft dirt and leaves.

With a flick of his sword to the side, Ryne rid it of any residue, and sheathed the weapon. "May Ilumni and his Battleguards keep you safe," he said in reverence.

Dizziness swirled through him for a brief moment, and he swayed. Sakari stepped forward to help, but Ryne waved him off. He'd grown used to these bouts of lightheadedness over the past few years. This one he could handle.

"What do you think?" Ryne nodded toward the corpse.

"No beast from the Rotted Forest delivered those wounds. And the only stench here is just death," Sakari said.

"A weapon?"

"None I can think of."

Ryne grunted his agreement. "And I see no auras around the body so no elements were used. Come let's see what else we find."

They searched the area but found nothing else out of place. Still baffled by what could have caused such grievous wounds, they left the stand and headed for home with Mariel still trailing them. With the sun beating down on them, they made a straight line for the sandstone edifice that marked Hagan's Inn.

"Let me guess," Dren said, an eyebrow arched. "You're going to let them know the error of their ways if this foolishness with Forian continues."

"Something like that," Ryne admitted, his voice even. "I think Mayor Bertram has downplayed just what kind of response the Tribunal would have if Mariel was harmed."

In short order, they reached the low wooden wall surrounding the village.

Dren slowed to a walk, his eyes focused toward the woods. He pointed. "Who's that out there?"

In that instant, a bestial roar pierced the humid afternoon air. Ryne's head whipped toward the sound, the same direction in which Dren, foot raised in an unfinished step, still pointed.

A boy stood frozen amongst the brush and long grass. The large teak, mahogany, and rosewood trees in the forest before him shook with such violence a rain of leaves fell.

"Kahkon?" Ryne said under his breath, cold fingers of dread slithering down his spine as he squinted at the skinny youth.

A huge beast, at least five the times the size of a large wolf, leaped from the dark woods. The aura about the creature shone with an obsidian blackness instead of its normal gray. Fluids dripped from raw, pink flesh and dark fur splotched black with decay. The infected lapra reared up on four of its six legs like a mantis preparing to attack. A wide, snout of a muzzle and forepaws tipped with sharp claws flashed. Before Kahkon could react, the beast snatched him by a leg. Kahkon screamed. A sound that brought shivers sliding down Ryne's back. With the same speed it struck, the lapra disappeared back into the trees, the boy a ragdoll in its mouth.

Chapter 2

Screams and cries from the villagers who witnessed the taking jarred Ryne into action. "Go!" he yelled to Sakari and Dren. "Fetch Lenka and Keevo. And gather several other hunters from the woods."

"What about Mariel?" Sakari gestured toward the woman.

"I'll deal with her. Go! Go!"

"No, Master Waldron. The elders, the villagers...you have to calm them," Dren implored, his eyes frantic.

"The boy comes first," Ryne snapped. He rounded on Dren, towering over him like a great cliff, his eyes steel. "I'll be damned if I have his blood on my hands. If I ever had a son, he'd be like Kahkon. I won't stand by—"

Dren grabbed at Ryne's arm. His hands trembled. "You don't understand, Master Waldron. The way Forian been going at them the last few days, they'll attack Mariel for sure with this. You know how it was during the War of Remnants. The Tribunal will kill everyone if we harm Mariel. I have a wife, sons...Master Waldron. Please. Look, if we're to save Kahkon, we can't afford for them to go traipsing into the Fretian now anyway. We'd be sure to lose the lapra's tracks. And if they go after Mariel, there'll be nowhere to hide from the Tribunal's wrath." Tears welled up in the scoutmaster's eyes.

Agonized by the need to save Kahkon, Ryne clenched his fists. Deep down, he knew Dren was right. Kahkon's survival meant a lot to him, but so did the rest of Carnas. He couldn't dream of sacrificing one for the other. Both needed him. As harsh as it sounded to himself, right now, staving off whatever malice resided in Carnas must take precedence. He needed to rely on Sakari and the others to find the tracks in time.

Torn, Ryne pulled his arm away from the scoutmaster. "Fine, fine," he whispered, his voice hoarse. "You two go. Gather the others. I'll inform the elders and settle the people down before I come. Sound the horn when you find the tracks. Sakari." Their gazes locked. "Do not fail."

"Thank you, Master Waldron," Dren said reverently.

Without a word, Sakari bowed and ran off with Dren following on his heels. Sakari weaved his way amongst frantically pointing villagers who'd crowded the hard-packed dirt road surrounded by Carnas' wooden homes. As he raced by, he gestured to two men in armor that matched his. One was a gray-haired, wiry man with a horn at his hip, and the other, a grizzle-faced hunter whose arms were all sinew. They ran after Sakari toward the woods.

Broad back and legs stiff from fighting the urge to chase after them, Ryne turned and stalked in the opposite direction toward Hagan's Inn. Villagers still pointed and a few young boys had climbed onto a roof and were gazing out toward the Fretian Woods. Concerned chatter flowed among the throngs on the road.

The door to Hagan's Inn burst open. Mayor Bertram, Hagan, and several other members from Carnas' village Council rushed outside the three-storied sandstone building. Ryne strode to meet them.

"What's happening?" Bertram's scarred face was gaunt and grim. His one good eye scanned the panicked crowd. His left arm, which ended at the elbow, moved on its own accord.

Hagan waddled just behind him, chest heaving, shirt so tight about his barrel-shaped belly it appeared as if it would burst open with his next breath. "Has another body been found?" He popped his pipe into the corner of his mouth and kneaded giana leaves into the bowl.

A flurry of questions spilled from the other Council members. Ryne lifted his hand, and a reluctant silence followed as villagers gathered in a respectful band around the elders.

"No, there hasn't been another body," Ryne said, feeling a great weight on his chest as he thought about the boy's small shape hanging from the beast's jaws. "But an infected lapra took Kahkon."

Gasps sounded from all around. Standing well over everyone, Ryne took in their wide–eyed expressions and animated gestures.

"An infected lapra?" Bertram repeated. "Here? You certain? How…What's it doing here? The Rot is hundreds of miles away. And the wards…"

Several other elders seconded Bertram's opinion.

Ryne shook his head. "It doesn't need to make sense. That's what took the boy. You can ask anyone who saw." Some Council members did as he suggested. In turn, Ryne graced them with a glare. "Listen, you can stay here and continue to squabble about Mariel's intentions. Or who or what killed those men we found near the kinai orchards. Or about what took the other eight villagers. I'll have none of it. Before Kahkon ends up like them, I'm going after the boy. I've already sent Sakari to gather a few others for the task."

A gravelly voice called from the crowd, "Mariel sent the beast." All eyes shifted to the baldheaded man. Baker Forian wiped greasy hands on an apron dark with stains. "She took those who we be missing too."

Ryne raised his brow. "You have proof of this?"

Forian sucked in his paunch as he held himself erect. "I seen her speak to plains lapras with my own two." He pointed at his beady eyes. "They ran off without bothering the woman once. If that not be proof then what be?"

Several people gave doubtful grumbles, while others sounded as if they expected such an occurrence. Forian's face flushed, but from his eyes, Ryne could tell the man believed what he said. Ryne frowned. Could Mariel have taken the villagers? The thought had crossed his mind before, but he'd yet to find proof. Yet, what made him more uncertain was the chance she might have an ability to commune with beasts similar to Sakari. He'd never seen anyone who possessed a skill comparable to his companion.

Despite his doubts, Ryne decided on caution. If he left now without knowing where the beast headed, the last mistake he needed was to unwittingly lead Mariel to the hunters' location. Not to mention the consequences if he didn't find a way to calm the murderous intent Forian had stirred up.

"But she's a Devout," someone from the gathered crowd shouted.

"If she be a Devout, she wouldn't be involved in such things," Forian insisted.

Mayor Bertram scoffed. "If, indeed. We've argued all day about whether she's a Devout. I tend to believe differently. If only they would see it." He regarded the other elders with his good eye narrowed. "I've yet to see a high priestess without their guards or their uniform." All, except Hagan, avoided his gaze.

The innkeeper blew a puff of perfumed giana smoke into the air. "She bears the Lightstorm insignia. And—"

A wail broke out from the back of the crowd. Murmurs drifted through the villagers. A path opened between them to reveal a middle-aged woman stumbling toward the elders— Kahkon's mother, Lara. Several men helped hold up the weeping woman. Dark circles ringed her eyes. Her disheveled clothing appeared as if she'd thrown on any scrap she could find when she received the news.

Lara's body convulsed. "My Kahkon. My poor Kahkon," she bawled.

One man bent close and spoke into Lara's ear. Her head rose, and her gaze ran over the Council. They regarded her with pity. She scrubbed at her tear-streaked face as she shambled into the circle of village elders. When she saw Ryne, a faint, hopeful expression spread across her face before more sobs tore from her throat, and she swooned.

Ryne stepped forward and caught her. In her hand, she cradled one of the books he'd given to Kahkon—the boy's favorite—*When the Gods Walked Among Us,* the title read. Kahkon had a love for the old stories and would often say he dreamed of being one of the gods. In his dreams, he said Ryne was one of his Battleguards, protecting him as he did Carnas. Ryne's chest tightened with the memory.

"I'll return your boy safely, Miss Lara. I promise. As soon as Sakari sends word he's found the beast's trail." Ryne held her upright so he could peer down into her grief–ridden eyes.

Lara's legs steadied, and she craned her neck. Her bloodshot eyes darted back and forth, peering into his, hope radiating from them. "I, I know you will, Master Waldron," she said, her voice tremulous. "He's my only boy. I told him, you know. I told him about the dead men they been finding. I told him stay away from the woods, but you know Kahkon. He loves the trees. Why me, Master Waldron? Why my boy?"

"I don't know, but I intend to find out." Ryne released his hold on Kahkon's mother.

"It be Mariel's fault all this be happening," another person yelled from the crowd.

"Look at the kinai crops. It's her fault we haven't had constant rains the last few months for a proper harvest. In the middle of the rainy season. And this year's fruit been sour besides. The storm gods punish us like in the days of the Shadowbearer."

Ryne eyed the large warehouse a few feet from where they stood. The normally fist–sized kinai fruit stacked in buckets in front the building were withered and brown.

A second voice joined in. "The old blood still runs strong among us in Ostania. We'd never lay with daemons or wolves like the Granadians do."

"Praise be to the true god, Humelen," a third voice yelled.

"It's because they partake in flesh instead of the purity of the land," another villager shouted.

"The Granadians brought ruin to Ostania twice," Forian announced. "And they will again. Let them keep their lecherous ways across the sea. It be them made all manner of monsters descend upon our lands. I say burn that bitch, Mariel, before she can make half–wolf children or any other daemon spawn who grow up worshiping the shade. Who be with me?"

Bloodthirsty shouts ruptured the air until the uproar grew to an incomprehensible din. Lara began wailing again. Men and women reached for swords or clubs, and metal rasped on leather. Those who did not already clench weapons shook their fists.

"Just head on out, Master Waldron," old, toothless Sanada pleaded. "Sure as fleas to a dog, she follows you. My sons can go before you do. The rest of us can trail her. You all turn back and she be ours for the taking."

Ryne ignored the man and the nods and murmurs of approval.

A smile curled onto Mayor Bertram's lips. Ryne's Scripts shifted like the tentative brush of a new lover's fingers against his skin. For an instant, Ryne thought he saw the man's aura flash to a darker shade, but it was gone so fast he dismissed the sight as a trick of the day's heat. Bertram's and Forian's gazes met for a brief instant before Forian gave a subtle nod.

Ryne wanted nothing more than to make his way to the woods to help in the search for the boy. Yet, he'd seen this coming for weeks now. He'd hoped the Council meetings would have given Bertram pause in his efforts to stir up the people. But the hateful seeds sown by Bertram through Forian had taken stronger root. If he did nothing, and they continued to grow, someone would indeed be bold enough to attack Mariel. If only Bertram wasn't so blinded by hate.

"Stop!" Ryne's basso voice thundered over the riotous crowd. The din dwindled to a murmur. A few village folk standing close to him retreated several steps. "Listen to yourselves. When have any of you seen what you speak of? When have you seen any man control the weather? Daemon spawn? When have any of you seen a Granadian or a Devout give birth to or create a shadeling?"

He met their heated expressions with an icy scowl, daring anyone to answer.

"Because you don't see a thing doesn't mean it didn't happen," Baker Forian yelled.

Ryne gave the man a stare that could curdle milk. "Forian, when has anyone you've known witnessed any such occurrence? What is it but poison you've been spreading for years? Now even more so when this woman has shown up. You claimed to have proof of her ill intentions, but you provided none beyond your word. And that, in itself, can be called to account due to your own ways. Believe me, if you can prove to me here and now she's involved, I'll deal with her myself."

"Her speaking to lapras not be proof?" Forian retorted.

"You've seen Sakari speak to all manner of beasts, does that make him evil? A child stealer? A creator of shadelings?" Ryne shook his head at the absurdity of his own questions. Everything he'd read agreed the shade's beastly minions couldn't be created in this realm. When Forian didn't answer, Ryne carried on. "Miss Corten often spoke to her flowers. Old Sanada speaks to his dogs and the rats and pheasants." Sanada shifted uneasily as Ryne continued. "Hagan likes to chatter to the birds. Are they evil? Does it mean they were involved in the creature taking the boy?"

Red–faced, Forian dipped his head and avoided Ryne's cold stare. "All I know be what I saw her do. And it be said when the rot leaves the forest, the shade will walk the land." He peered at the faces around him. "Well, the rot left the forest. An infected lapra. If what she did not be of the shade then what be?" He paused for effect. "This be the first time I seen any beasts leave the Rot. And it happens when she be here, after she speaks to the same type of creature." He turned his hands palms up as if the conclusions were inescapable. "I don't call that chance." A few in the crowd nodded their agreement.

Concerned mutters followed from the elders before Hagan spoke up. "You should be careful what you say, Forian." He kept his voice low, but it still carried. "We wouldn't want wind of words she might consider blasphemy to get back to her ears." He peered in the direction of Mariel's last camp.

"Why should we care what she thinks is blasphemy?" Bertram shrugged, his one–eyed gaze taking in everyone. "Even if she is a Devout, none of us here worship her gods."

Murmurs of agreement joined the nods, steadily increasing. Someone else yelled Humelen was the true god.

Glowering, Ryne drew himself up, causing those nearby to take a few steps back as he loomed even larger. "Most of you here have been a part of the War of Remnants. You helped drive the last of the shadelings from your lands. Yet, your lands wouldn't be your own right now if not for the same people you rebuke. Take a look around you." He pointed at the rolling plains, then he gestured to the squat wooden buildings along the alleys and lanes within Carnas. "Look at your children, your neighbors, your friends." He kept his eyes fixed on the villagers until they did as he commanded. "Without Granadia's help, without the Devout," he grimaced even before he said the next bit, "without the Tribunal, you may not be here today. They saved you from the shade. Remember that."

The unrest died down.

"You be the reason we be here today," Hagan said, his voice quiet.

Bertram cocked his head to regard Ryne with his good eye. The burn scar tissue covering the left side of Bertram's face puckered, but he said nothing.

Ryne ignored Bertram's expression and continued, "The most important thing right now is seeing Kahkon to safety. Debate these outlandish stories and accusations another time. Return to your homes. Make sure your children are safe. No one is to venture near the Fretian Woods."

Few grumbled protests followed, but after a look at Ryne's hulking form and hardened face, the villagers dispersed in small groups. Ryne waited to make sure the village square was clear.

"A moment if you will, Master Waldron," Bertram said.

"Hagan and I would like to speak with you." He gestured toward the door of the inn.

"I've more important things to do," Ryne snapped. "As do you. You should be seeing to your people." He took in the mayor's glare with a look akin to frozen steel.

Bertram growled something under his breath and spun on his heels. The elders followed.

Ryne signaled to Vana and Vera. The serving women ambled over to him. "I need you two to take Miss Lara home. See to her needs and make sure she's comfortable."

"Yes, my Lord," Vana said.

Vera held out her hand. "Lord Waldron, take this with you." She handed a pouch to him, and he leaned forward to see what it contained. "It's the best kinai we could find. We had the mender make a paste just for you. It may also be useful when you find the boy."

"You should eat some now too," Vana added. She tiptoed and brushed her hand on the scars that striped the left side of his face. "There's never anything wrong with a little extra energy." She gave him a sweet smile.

Ryne sighed. He almost told them again he was no lord, but he knew his words would come and go like a fluttering breeze. Instead, he accepted their gift, acknowledged them both with a nod, and admired their shapes as they curtsied and hurried off with Miss Lara in tow.

A hunter's horn wailed from within the woods.

Ryne dashed off toward the sound. Villagers scrambled out of his way as he bounded along the main road before he veered off into one of the many alleys, startling a few dogs foraging among garbage, the foul odor of piss and other undesirable waste permeating the air—the result of almost two weeks without rain. He leaped over the clogged drains and past the homes that lined the alleys, his leather boots making soft, rhythmic thuds as he ran. More than once, children at play jumped from his path. Emerging from Carnas' eastern exit, he dodged past the gate in the low wooden wall. When he glanced out to his left, he growled.

Mariel watched him from across the plains. As usual, she maintained a distance where he couldn't see her aura.

Ryne focused ahead and made a straight path toward the Fretian Woods. As he ran, he took a quick peek over his shoulder.

Mariel followed

Chapter 3

Irmina Nagel studied the giant man racing across the grassy dips and slopes of the terrain. Just watching the giant with the sun beating on him while only the slightest of breezes whispered through the air made her wish for a drink of water. With the back of her hand, she flicked away dark strands of hair stuck to her face and wiped at sweat streaming down her brow.

The thick fescue and blue and red flowering brush of the Orchid Plains offered little resistance to the man's massive legs. His two–handed greatsword's wide scabbard bounced on his thigh before he brought his hand down and kept it in place. He ate up the distance in great strides, three times a normal man's full stretched leap.

She kept a careful eye on him and his tattoos. With his every move, they glinted like precious stones where they caught the sunlight. Any change in direction could be an attempt to capture her again. He'd tried three times since she came to Carnas, and she'd quickly learned to add more distance than her master had advised.

Birds fluttered from his path into the sparse trees, their sharp squawks announcing their displeasure. The one time he'd looked over his shoulder was his only acknowledgment of her existence, but she knew better than to think he forgot about her presence. As he closed in on the woods, Irmina's vigilance increased. The man's strange bodyguard and two others had passed that way. Soon after, she'd heard the horn from the same direction.

Are they trying to save the boy or hunt the creature down? She frowned. Even she wouldn't want to confront the infected lapra within the forest's confines. Her brief peek into the creature's head revealed a mind as decayed as the rest of its body. The beast refused her attempt to command it to release the boy. Despite the day's warmth, a shiver ran through her.

When she saw the lapra spring from the woods, she'd been tempted to try save Kahkon in a more direct manner. She almost did, before she realized it would be a fatal mistake. The giant man would see the power she used. High Shin Jerem had been explicit in his orders. At no time should she reveal herself to the man. Not if she wished to live.

Another question nagged at Irmina. What was the boy doing near the woods anyway? She'd sent a warning to the mayor about the golden–haired woman and the lapra's presence. Why would they still allow the children—or anyone unprotected for that matter—to venture near the forest after those who already went missing? Her brow puckered. *Unless Kahkon didn't deliver my message. Maybe he forgot? No, he wouldn't. Maybe, he didn't understand?* But that didn't seem likely.

Two things surprised her since coming to Carnas in her guise as Mariel the Devout. The first was many of the Ostanian youth in the village spoke Granadian to some extent. The second was the giant man had taught them. Her stories about the gods mesmerized Kahkon, and he never missed a chance to visit her each day. She'd promised him more stories if he took her message directly to the mayor. He hadn't returned since.

She wondered if the reason for Kahkon's absence bore any relation to the odd way the villagers acted of late. When she first arrived, most paid proper reverence to her Devout title, although without the typical uniform, she had nothing but her insignia of the sun encased in a halo to show as proof of her stature. Over the last few weeks, their outlook changed. She noticed a peculiar, abrasive attitude from the village folk since they found the last few dead bodies in the kinai glades and their own people disappeared. Each day since, the number of visitors dwindled until only Kahkon frequented her campsites in secret. *Do they think I'm somehow responsible for the deaths or the missing villagers?*

At first, she thought it might be someone among them who knew she was not who she claimed to be. She'd entertained the notion someone had contacts within the Tribunal and informed the villagers she didn't represent the Tribunal's interests here in Ostania. She'd quickly dismissed the idea as ludicrous. High Shin Jerem assured her no one in Granadia would know of her presence here. One did not doubt the High Shin.

That left the recent murders and disappearances. Surely, they didn't think she killed those men or took the others. If so, why? Could the village folk believe a Devout capable of carrying out such crimes? The savagery of Granadian politics was a thing long dead, with nothing amounting to more than petty squabbles over the last three decades. That past was the very reason the Tribunal ruled and Devout were appointed. The Tribunal's rise and Streamean worship ensured all in Granadia walked the path of light. The idea of a Devout engaging in such heinous actions was so foreign to her as to be unfathomable. If they knew her true identity, she could've understood this train of thought. But her disguises had never failed on any mission.

All this brought her to the golden–haired woman in the woods. Irmina had only gained a glimpse of her twice, but several bodies were found in the same general vicinity soon after. She'd ruled out coincidence and sent a warning to the mayor. If only she could confirm its delivery.

Regardless, she would be even more careful. She needed to keep in mind these people were less civilized than she was accustomed. Who knew what other strange beliefs they entertained? If the giant and his bodyguard were a good guide, these Ostanians possessed capabilities she would be a fool to underestimate.

Irmina licked her lips at the salty taste of sweat as she

picked her way through the brush and sparse trees. A light breeze blew, but offered little relief from the humid air. Ahead, the giant man continued his run toward the woods, his strides steady, the sun and the hot air appearing to have little to no effect.

"Find the man, the High Shin says. When you do, you must convince him of your need, he says. He must return with you to Granadia. Pwah. I should've known it wouldn't be so simple when you told me I could never allow him to see me use my abilities." Irmina ground her teeth.

As if this wasn't difficult enough, Jerem had assured her the time would come here in Ostania when she would face the hardest decision she would ever make in her life. He'd warned her whatever she chose would prove crucial in what path she took and would scar her for life. As if she didn't already bear enough scars. Every moment spent in this backward land made her regret taking on this mission. If not for Jerem's insistence that this was a required step in the completion of her training, she may have refused. For her, graduation meant another toehold toward vengeance.

The thought brought a shudder through her and sparked a memory of her as a child when she received the news of her family's murder—her mother, father, brothers and her sister lying face down in pools of blood. The despair and loneliness she felt before the Dorns adopted her arose fresh and raw. She brushed tears from her eyes as she remembered the blinding rage she burned with a year ago when she discovered the part the Dorns played in her family's demise.

Thinking of her lost family and the Dorns served to prompt her feelings for Ancel. He was part of the reason she'd cried then. For the love the Dorns had taken from her not once but three times. Despite her hatred for Ancel's parents, a longing for his touch, to see his emerald eyes, to see his carefree smile, eased through her. With any luck, he'd gotten over her by now. It wouldn't make what she needed to do much easier, but it might help.

She squeezed her eyes tight as she wished she could rewrite her last words and instead tell him how much she loved him. She wished she could have told him the truth of her mission. She wished she could've told him the truth about his parents.

Her last thought grated her insides. The people who raised her as their own, who she'd come to love and care for since she lost her family, had been revealed as frauds. Murderous frauds, who, to this day, clung to their plots. How many others knew what occurred? How many more were involved? She would weed them out one by one for as long as she lived. And let them feel the pain she endured.

Life and love are brutal teachers. Learn, adjust, and survive. Or die. Those are your choices. I choose life. She repeated Jerem's mantra to herself as she did every day since her discovery.

Irmina grasped at the slim sword in its sheath at her waist. Her hand shook with strain. The weapon was not what a priestess typically carried, and although not quite as effective as a regiment of guards, it served its purpose to deter most bandits. More than that, the sword was once her mother's weapon. Those foolish enough to ignore her blade because she was a woman soon learned their mistake. Remembering her training, she opened the cold place deep in her mind and shoved her emotions there until they dwindled. For this mission, she could afford no distractions.

Her master had given her so little information, and the villagers even less. None she interviewed gave up the names of either the giant or his bodyguard with the disconcerting silver eyes. Not even the children. Their faces became guarded every time she mentioned the two men.

When she first saw them, she hadn't given the giant's companion much thought. He appeared of no consequence. He had typical Ostanian swarthy skin and sandy hair, his height well over six feet. This was before she saw him move. He never appeared to touch the ground, his sinuous frame gliding like oil across a smooth surface. His eyes too, were odd, like silver flashes of frictionless mercury.

His master, the eight–foot giant with the tattoos, appeared to live up to her master's description as the more dangerous of the two. To some extent, she agreed. She'd observed them in their daily sparring sessions when the giant would win three fights for each one he lost. They fought with a grace and skill that would shame the best Weaponmasters in Eldanhill. Yet, for all the bigger man's skill, something about his guardian made her skin crawl.

Irmina found herself peering toward the tree line ahead as she thought about Silvereyes. As she did, she noticed the glint from the tattoos no longer bounced rhythmically.

The giant stood at the forest's edge staring at her.

Irmina ducked and slid behind a tree. If he entertained any thoughts to chase after her once again, she would make sure he realized she was not easy game.

Chapter 4

Ancel Dorn brushed his hand against his beige coat's breast pocket. Despite knowing the words by heart, the letter he kept there tempted him to take it out and read for the thousandth time. He clenched his reins tighter in his fist. *Nine hundred and ninety nine is good enough.*

His mare crested the hill lined on both sides by small fields and the Greenleaf Forest that dominated this part of the Whitewater Falls region. Miles to the right and north, beyond the forest, the Kelvore Mountains stretched their broad shoulders and snowcapped peaks. Straight ahead on the rutted road, Eldanhill spread before him and Mirza Faber.

The town's white and yellow brick buildings glinted in the early morning sunlight. Dominating the town's center, the square clock tower of the Streamean temple jutted up at least ten stories above the slate and tile roofs of the other sandstone and granite structures. Townsfolk bustled down the wide, yet already crowded, Eldan Road, appearing more like small colorful insects than people.

The distant buzz of a thousand conversations, clopping hooves, trundling wagon and dray wheels, and hundreds of daily activities played a familiar rhythm. Among them rang the clang of smithies and stonemasons, the whir and rattle of the many windmills along the Kelvore River, the receding roar from the

Whitewater Falls to the northeast, and the bird song and chatter of small animals within the Greenleaf.

The clamor and his surroundings brought a soothing sensation along Ancel's shoulder and neck. An unusually chill wind that smelled of rain streamed his cloak out behind him. Ancel shivered and glanced to Mirza who rode the chestnut stallion thudding a slow rhythm a few feet away.

Mirza tilted to one side, grabbing at the pages of the book he'd been reading as the wind whipped at the pages. He snatched for his reins and pommel, barely managing to prevent himself from falling. Ancel chuckled.

"That wasn't funny," Mirza said as he righted himself. His skinny legs, in the narrow pants he favored, squeezed against the stallion's side. The fitted coat he wore matched Ancel's own except for the book and pen insignia stitched to the lapel. Ancel's emblem was a silver sword.

"Not funny to you," Ancel replied. "But if you sat where I am and saw your arms and legs fly all over you'd be laughing too."

Mirza passed a hand through his rust–colored hair. "I guess I would." He smiled.

"You know, if you studied at night you wouldn't need to cram the next day."

"I did study," Mirza protested. "But I'm not like you. I need to refresh the morning of a test so I don't forget anything."

Ancel shrugged. "The test will be simple enough."

"Easy for you to say," Mirza grumbled. "You've taken it already."

"It was simple then too."

"Well, if it's so easy, how about helping? Ask me a few questions." Mirza leaned over to hand him the book.

Ancel shooed him off. "I don't need it. Just tell me what you want me to ask."

Mirza straightened his back. He rubbed a thumb on the reddish stubble growing from his chin. "How about the gods? And Mater?"

Seeing Mirza touch his beard made Ancel's own prickly growth itch. "You know, that's a pretty broad area." Ancel scratched at the offending sprigs of hair under his chin. "Here, I'll try to be specific and start with something easy."

Mirza nodded, hands fidgeting on the pommel of his saddle.

A few moments passed. Ancel said nothing. He stared off to the east where he could make out the rust colored Red Ridge Mountains beyond where the land dipped toward the Kelvore River.

Frowning, Mirza eyed him. "Well?"

"Well, close that," Ancel said, his head gesturing to the still open book in his friend's hand.

"Oh!" Mirza flipped the book shut.

"Uh, huh." Ancel gave his friend a wry look. "You just happened to have the chapter on religion open."

Mirza glowered at him. "Ask your questions already."

"Name the gods and their titles." Ancel's lips twitched ever so slightly.

Eyes widening, Mirza stammered, "A–All their titles, and all the gods?"

"Fine. Name the major gods and the elements of Mater they represent."

"That's easy." Mirza beamed.

"Really?" Ancel lifted his brow.

Mirza's smile changed to a scowl. "Ilumni, Amuni, Bragni and Rituni, the gods of Streams. Humelen, Liganen and Kinzanen, the gods of Forms. Hyzenki and Aeoli, the gods of Flows. There."

"Good, but not quite right" Ancel said, feeling a little sorry for his earlier sarcasm.

"What? They're all correct."

"Aeoli's a goddess," Ancel said with a bemused smirk.

Mirza groaned.

"Here, I'll ask you the first question you will see on the test, but you need to answer exactly as Teacher Calestis wrote or else she'll mark it wrong."

Intense concentration creased Mirza's brows.

"What's Mater?"

Mirza squinted and stroked his stubble with his thumb. After a few more moments, he said, "Mater is the core elemental power which exists within everything. It makes up the three elements the gods represent and their individual essences." He looked over for Ancel's approval.

"Go on," Ancel encouraged.

"Mater is more than just the elements driving our world. It drives all worlds," Mirza said with an air of finality. His face lit up.

Ancel smiled. That last bit was Teacher Calestis's favorite saying. "Excellent. What's the most important thing to practice and master before learning how to touch your Matersense?"

"Control. Emotional and physical."

"Perfect. Now—"

"Ancel," Mirza said, his smooth voice becoming serious. "Why're you back in the same class as me?"

Ancel absently brushed his breast pocket. "I told you. I failed the end of term test. They decided I needed to take religion and principles again."

"They're saying you failed it on purpose."

Ancel's eyes became slits. "Who?"

"The other students," Mirza said before he quickly averted his gray eyes. "They're saying you failed on purpose. Just so you could be in the same class where Irmina used to come meet you."

Ancel clenched his jaw, against both Mirza's words and the image of Irmina's golden brown eyes, her raven black hair, and her lithe form and shrugged. "They can say what they want. I failed. It's as simple as that. And what did I tell you about saying her name?"

"I, I'm sorry." Mirza scrunched up his face and shook his head. "I mean, no, I'm not."

Ancel glared at his friend. His hands tightened on his reins.

"Listen," Mirza pleaded. "You're my best friend. If I don't tell you, then who will? You've always been the smartest of us all. You'd have to be, to become the youngest trainee since… well ever. But after she left, you stopped caring. I hate watching you throw everything away."

"You don't know shit," Ancel spat.

"Burning shades, Ancel. I watch you every day. You practice the sword for the women. You bed as many as you can, and you daydream through class. That's not who you are. It's about time you moved on. She did. A year you said, remember? But you still pine over her. Now you risk failing classes again. All the things we dreamed about when we were young, playing at becoming Knights, of going off to join the legions, maybe one day crossing the Vallum of Light to help defend Granadia. It's all there for you. Why—"

"Just shut it," Ancel said his voice like ice. Another chill wind kicked up. This time he didn't shiver.

A sudden multitude of colors like miniature rainbows swirled through Ancel's vision as he stared toward Eldanhill. The hues appeared to jump across people and animals. They even stood out on the flock of birds in the near cloudless sky. He closed his eyes and rubbed his thumb and forefinger across his lids. When he opened his eyes, the colors were gone.

Ancel glanced toward Mirza, but his friend showed no reaction to what he'd seen. Instead, Mirza drew his cloak around himself, and his eyes focused on the rutted road ahead. Mirza ground his teeth, obviously still upset.

A soft coo made Ancel look toward the field to his right. Charra, his daggerpaw, loped through the short grass and shrubs. He stood as big as a bull, his head reaching almost to the withers of Ancel's mare. His shaggy, whitish fur was stained brown with whatever mischief he'd gotten himself into. Charra shook his broad muzzle, sending slobber flying into the air. The soft bone hackles, which extended around his neck and down his back in a bushy mane, swished.

"Where've you been, boy?" Ancel shouted, his mood a

little lighter at seeing his pet.

Charra's golden–eyed gaze swept to Ancel as he responded with a growl, crossed to the field on the other side road, and trotted a few feet ahead of their horses. Ancel shook his head. There was no accounting for Charra's moods.

Ancel returned to studying Mirza who still rode in silence. *If only you knew how right you are.* Ancel took a deep breath. Try as he might, he couldn't think without Irmina crossing his thoughts. His hand found its way to his coat pocket again.

"She wrote me the day she left, you know," Ancel said, his voice low.

Mirza looked at him from the corner of his eyes. "You mean the letter you read every day?"

Ancel cocked an eyebrow. "When'd you notice?"

"Hard not to," Mirza replied with a shake of his head. "We're only together every day. When you aren't touching that pocket of yours, you're lost in thought. Then sometimes when you think no one's watching, you pull the letter out and start reading."

"Why didn't you ask?"

Mirza gave him a rueful smile. "You promised to run me through if I ever mentioned her name."

"I'm surprised you listened for so long."

"You've never seen your own face when someone mentions the woman."

Ahead, Charra stopped to stare into the Greenleaf Forest. Ancel peered toward the tree line, but saw nothing. He dismissed it as part of Charra's recent habit of growling at shadows when he was in a foul mood.

"So what's in the letter?" Mirza asked.

"Not much. We'd spent the night together. When I woke, she was gone, and the letter was next to my pillow," Ancel answered absently, his gaze fixed on his daggerpaw. "The letter said she had to leave. That there was another." Ancel's chest throbbed with an almost physical pain. "She said she may never return to Eldanhill. That one day when I completed my studies and passed the trials, I'd understand. She just left me, as if I never mattered."

An uncomfortable silence followed. Somewhere among the trees, a bird began a mournful lament.

"Life and love are brutal teachers. Learn, adjust, and survive. Or die. Those are your choices. I choose life," Ancel said. He shrugged at Mirza's frown for his sudden statement. "Those were the words she repeated several times before she left. I think I'm now beginning to understand."

Ancel reached for the letter. At the same time, Charra growled, low and hard. His bone hackles rose into a ridge of hardened spikes, their edges sharp as a newly forged dagger, the ones about his neck almost a foot long before growing less dense and shorter as they tapered off near his tail. Ancel's gaze flitted from Charra to the woods. Brambles and bindweed snarled through the undergrowth and across stone outcrops beneath the trees. Red cedar and oak thrived. Except for the occasional sunlit patch, their canopies kept the forest in deep shadow.

"What's gotten into him now?" Mirza nodded to Charra.

"I don't know. He's been moodier than usual the last few days, growling at shadows and the like. But this…" Ancel stopped his mare. The horse pranced, and he rubbed its neck until it calmed. This had to be more than just Charra's mood.

"I've only seen him like this when we're hunting wolves." Mirza brought his mount next to Ancel's.

"Wolves wouldn't come this close to town," Ancel said.

Charra raised a shaggy foot and took one tentative step forward. He growled again, louder this time. The sound vibrated through Ancel. The horses' eyes rolled, and the animals whickered.

Stomach aflutter as he peered into the woods, Ancel frowned.

"Listen," Mirza said, his voice almost breathless.

Ancel did. His brow knitted tighter.

No birds sang. No animals chattered. The only sounds reaching them came from Eldanhill.

The wind rose again, a little stronger than before. A faint smell from some animal, long dead, reached them. This time Ancel found himself rubbing his arms from the chill.

Did a shadow just pass through that patch of sun? Ancel squinted at the spot within the woods, but he saw no other movement.

"Did you see that?" Mirza whispered, his question confirming what Ancel thought he saw.

Ancel nodded.

The breeze passed, and the air stilled. The silence remained for another moment before birdsong rose and other sounds from the woods resumed.

Charra whined, bone hackles softening and receding until they once again lay flat against his fur. He turned and loped toward Eldanhill.

Ancel and Mirza sat there for a moment more, their gazes still riveted on the dappled shadows.

Mirza broke their silence. "What do you think it was?"

"I don't know. But I wouldn't worry about it now." Ancel nodded toward Charra who continued toward Eldanhill. "He isn't."

"I guess." Mirza flapped his reins and started his stallion down the road.

Ancel followed, troubled by Charra's reaction and Mirza's earlier words about Irmina. As much as he wanted to return to his old self, he was not sure he could. *It's not like I asked to feel this way about her. It just happened. Somehow, I'll work this out. I think.*

Charra, on the other hand, was another issue. With his erratic behavior increasing, Ancel hoped his father wouldn't listen to the townsfolk and ask him to leave the daggerpaw at the winery. Not being able to bring him to school was one thing. To do without him in Eldanhill altogether was another entirely. Given a choice, he would rather not come to town at all if it meant leaving his daggerpaw behind.

Of course, not going to Eldanhill presented another set of problems. His need for female companionship would suffer. The thought made him remember today's rendezvous.

"By the way," Ancel said, "I'm supposed to meet with

Alys after school."

Mirza looked over his shoulder. "Is this your way of telling me you're shirking your duties again? We're supposed to be gathering kinai for Soltide and your father's winery later."

"I know," Ancel said. "But in case I lose track of time, I wanted you to know where to find me."

"Which means I *will* have to come find you."

Ancel snorted. "If that's what you think, then—"

"Here's what," Mirza interrupted. "I'll do it if you're willing to make a wager."

"If you want to lose more coin to me," Ancel shrugged, "Who am I to argue? So what's the bet?"

"Simple. I bet you'll think more with your cock than with your head. I know you won't be able to hold back. Not with Alys. So if I have to come get you, it'll cost you a gold hawk. If you manage on your own, I owe you two."

Ancel grinned. "There's no way I'll lose."

"We'll see."

They continued on their way to their classes at Eldanhill's Mystera.

Message From the Author

Creating this book was even more enjoyable than my first one, and I hope you enjoyed it. Again, I humbly ask that you venture onto Amazon and Goodreads and the like and review this book. This goes a long way to helping any author. Also it lets us know how you feel. After all, what are we without you, the reader? Nothing at all.

Don't forget to come visit my blog, terrycsimpson. wordpress.com and become a fan on my facebook page, TCSimpson on Facebook, if it so moves you. Insightful comments are always welcome. So come on, take the journey, help increase this vision of a whole new world. Below, you will find an excerpt from Etchings of Power.

Terry C. Simpson.

ERRY . SIMPSON

Acknowledgements

First, thanks to the Man upstairs.

A big thanks to my Speculative Collective Writing Group. Ted, my man, Ted. What can I say? Without your awesome beta reading and critiques this book would be a shell fo itself. Lee, thanks for your input on war strategy and making it better. Katie as always good with grammar. Elisa and Ed, I miss all you guys and gals.

A big thanks to another beta reader, Ann Cannaliato. Your diligent work on the writing site where me met was invaluable in shaping this work. I thank you from the bottom of my heart for bearing with me and setting your own work aside to read mine. And for backing me up and defending my writing.

As usual, another thanks to my editor D Kai Wilson–Viola. Your patience is a breath of fresh air.

Thank you to Valeri Douglas and Kai for putting together the Alexandria Publishing Group.

To my best friend Hughey, you know I can never forget you.

TERRY C. SIMPSON

Fantasy works from authors at Alexandria Publishing Group.

By David M Brown
Fezariu's Epiphany
By Valerie Douglas
Song of the Fairy Queen
The Coming Storm Series
Setting Boundaries
Not Magic Enough
The Coming Storm
A Convocation of Kings
By Paul Kater
Hilda the Wicked Witch series
Hilda the wicked witch
Hilda – Snow White revisited
Hilda – The Challenge
Hilda and Zelda
Hilda – Cats
Hilda – Lycadea
Hilda – Back to School
Hilda – Dragon Master
By Stephen H. King

THE SHADOWBEARER

Cataclysm: Return of the Gods
Ascension: Return of the Gods
By Jonathan Gould

Doodling
Flidderbugs
Magnus Opum

www.ingramcontent.com/pod-product-compliance
Lightning Source LLC
Chambersburg PA
CBHW071253170626
46809CB00001B/206